Love Me Once
Love Me Twice
Montana Cowboys 1

Sandy Sullivan

EROTIC ROMANCE

Secret Cravings Publishing

www.secretcravingspublishing.com

A Secret Cravings Publishing Book

Erotic Romance

Love Me Once, Love Me Twice
Montana Cowboys 1
Copyright © 2010 by Sandy Sullivan
Print ISBN: 978-1-936653-38-6

First E-book Publication: December 2010
First Print Publication: March 2011
Cover design by Beth Walker
Edited by Trena Hayes and Ariana Gaynor
All cover art and logo copyright © 2010 by Secret Cravings Publishing

PUBLISHER
Secret Cravings Publishing
www.secretcravingspublishing.com

Dedication

This book is dedicated to my fans. You've stood by me through my changes in publishers and my experimentation with other genres, but it all comes back to the cowboys.

I love you all!

LOVE ME ONCE LOVE ME TWICE

Montana Cowboys 1

Sandy Sullivan

Copyright © 2010

Chapter One

Red Rock, Montana
Established 1895

The headlights reflected the white letters on the green sign, bright as day, even though darkness shrouded the countryside. Snow fell in flurries heavy enough to make it difficult to see and stay on the roadway. Deep ruts in the snow gave Natalie Bennington something to follow, so they obviously hadn't plowed the road in a while.

"I never will understand why in the hell they put the sign for town clear out here," she grumbled. "It's still a good five miles in yet." A deep sigh left her lips. "I sure as hell never thought I'd be back here. Fifteen years is a long time to be gone. I can't walk away from Gram though. Not after what she's been through."

The tires spun as she tried to go a little faster.

"Wow. These roads are bad."

Her grip on the steering wheel tightened, turning her knuckles white.

"I haven't really driven in snow in ages, well, nothing like Montana snow anyway."

A small hill loomed in front of her, and she knew if she didn't speed up to some degree, she'd never make it up. With a miniscule amount of pressure on the gas pedal, she started a slow climb.

Halfway up, the tires started to spin, and the back end of the car began to fishtail.

"Oh no." The ditch to her right loomed from the darkness like the gaping holes of hell. "Shit, shit, shit!" Barbed wire fencing stretched from one pole to another just beyond the backside of the trench, and without a doubt, she knew the gully had her name on it. The back of the car slid faster and faster toward the right while she struggled to keep it on the road, to no avail. Seconds later, she heard a dull thud and a loud crack as the rear hit the dirt, slipping into the crevice. The next thing she knew, she was staring through the windshield at the falling snow while the beams from her headlights reflected nothing—only disappeared into inky blackness.

"Now what the hell am I going to do? It's still a hell of a long walk to town, and it's snowing like crazy," she grumbled and slammed her fist against the steering wheel. This trip started out bad and continued worsening the farther she got from "civilization". The truck stops stunk, the food sucked, and the motel beds couldn't have one ounce of padding left in them because she felt every spring and every bulge. The truckers ogled, flirted, and propositioned at each gas station and bathroom stop. In addition, the weather hadn't helped, snowing almost constantly. The highway department closed the interstate for two days—two days of dealing with lonely men and very few women at a motel she wasn't sure didn't rent rooms by the hour, outside Coeur D'Alene, Idaho. Her cell phone battery died earlier in the day, and she'd forgotten her car charger at home.

I should never have come on this trip, but Grandma needs me.

On the verge of tears, she bit her lip and shook her head. She could give into the frustration and aggravation while no one could see her. *One, two, three, four, five.*

Too many times, she reminded her students to count to five before they did anything while angry.

It really doesn't help a whole lot.

Headlights appeared, coming from the direction of town.

"Great! Maybe it's someone who can help me get my damned car out of this hole."

The door handle felt cold under her hand when she tried to pull it and open the heavy panel. Gravity wasn't her friend, even though she pushed with everything she had, it wouldn't budge.

"Hello? Anyone in there?" A deep baritone yelled while he tapped on the window.

"Yes! I can't get the door open."

"Hang on," he said and disappeared for a second.

"Wait! Where are you going? Don't leave me in here. I'll freeze to death."

"I'm not leavin', honey. Hold tight."

The endearment sent a little flutter in her stomach. No one called her honey or darlin'. Then again, this was Montana, home of the gentleman cowboy, where every female was honey, darlin', or sweetheart.

Metal squeaked and groaned, but the driver's side finally opened.

"Hey there. In a bit of a pickle, huh?"

"You could say so, yes."

"Can you crawl out while I hold this open?"

"I think so."

The snow crunched under her boots when her feet touched. The man let the door bang shut behind her.

"Thank you," she said, trying not to slide into the hole behind her.

"You're welcome. How'd you end up in there anyway?"

"My car fishtailed in the snow and in the gap I went. What's it look like?"

"Easy. Just askin'," he replied, pushing his black cowboy hat back on his head.

"Can you help me get it out?"

"Sorry, darlin'. I have four-wheel drive, but it doesn't matter. Your car ain't goin' anywhere. The drive train snapped."

"You're kidding."

"Nope, I saw it in two pieces when I drove up. Are you sure you ain't hurt?"

"I'm fine other than bruised pride."

"Where are you goin' and I'll give you a lift?"

"Into Red Rock. My grandmother's actually."

"You ain't from here are you?"

"Not anymore, why?"

"You used to be?"

"Yes, actually. I was born and raised here until my parents moved us out of town about fifteen years ago. My gram still lives here."

"What's your name?"

She frowned, clamping her lips closed, afraid she already gave out too much information. If the man happened to be a psycho or something, she'd probably already told him enough to find her.

As if he could read her mind, he said, "I'm not some weirdo, just a good 'ole country boy. Born and raised here and trying to help a lady in distress."

"Are you serious? I don't believe you." She cocked her head to the side, studying his features the best she could in the dim light, "My name is Natalie Bennington."

"Nat? The same Nat in the band?"

"No one calls me Nat."

"I did, or should I say *we* use to. Me and Kale anyway."

"Cade Weston?"

"One and the same." He shifted from foot to foot, stomping his feet a couple of times. "You know, I'd love to stand out here and chitchat, but I'm about to freeze to death. The roads are impassible if you don't have chains or four-wheel drive. I'll grab your stuff and take you home."

Once he retrieved her suitcase from her car, she followed him to the passenger side of the truck, and asked, "What are you doing driving in this if the roads are so bad?"

The door opened with a lift of the handle, and she could finally see his face a little—only enough to see the corners of his mouth lift in a smile and a flash of white teeth. She still couldn't see his eyes, but from what she remembered, he had the prettiest baby blues of anyone she knew.

"Shootin' pool and havin' a good time. It is Saturday."

"I should have known."

The wind howled outside the windows, but the heater blast warm air throughout the vehicle. Snow swirled in the beams from the headlights, almost obliterating the view outside.

"Wow. It's really coming down out there," he said, once inside, shutting the door.

When he took his hat off and tossed it onto the back seat, she got a glimpse of the brown locks she remembered. A moment later, he fixed his gaze on her, and she forgot to breathe.

Holy shit!

A five o'clock shadow of whiskers covered his jaw, making him look a little rugged and a whole lot handsome.

He put the truck in drive and slowly pulled around her car.

"They won't tow my car, will they?"

"No. It should be fine until tomorrow. The snow is supposed to stop later tonight, and the plow should be through early."

"I hope they don't bury it."

A warm chuckle left his mouth, sending goose bumps flittering across her arms.

Cade and Kale were two of the most popular boys in school. Somewhat opposites in looks, Cade with brown hair and blue eyes, and Kale with dark brown hair and brown eyes, they kept many a girl twittering behind their hands in hopes of a little attention from one or the other, or both.

"Don't worry. If they do, I have a shovel."

The lights of town came into view a short moment later, but her grandmother's house was still a few miles away. Red Rock, Montana hadn't changed much in the time she'd been gone. A few businesses she remembered were now gone, and a few new ones took their place. Johnny's Gas Station still occupied the corner of Olive and First. A chain store grocery replaced Smith's. The Hometown Feed hadn't moved. Nevertheless, right now, all the doors were closed tight and nothing stirred except the wind and snow.

"What are you doing now, here in Red Rock?" she asked, curious about the man he turned into after school.

"Same thing I've always done. Work horses." A quick glance in her direction had her shivering. "And tryin' to stay out of trouble. Not easy to do in this town sometimes."

What the hell is wrong with me? Yeah, he's gorgeous, but I'm not looking to get into a relationship with anyone, much less someone in Red Rock.

"True. Have you managed to do that so far? Stay out of trouble, I mean."

A wiry smile crossed his mouth. "Not so much. I stole a car a long time ago. Well, I should say we did, Kale and I."

"Wow! Really? You didn't come across so rebellious to me."

"Luckily, the car belonged to a neighbor, and they didn't press charges since it made it back to them in one piece. If I remember right, you left town before I really got into trouble. Where did y'all go anyway?"

"Oregon. My dad got transferred after the plant closed here."

"Must have been hard."

"Yeah. Not easy making new friends at fifteen after you've spent your entire life in a town no bigger than a suburb of Portland." One shoulder lifted in a shrug. "I survived and even made some close friends."

"I heard about your grandfather. I'm sorry."

The sight of him sitting across the truck from her made her wonder what he thought about her all those years ago. "It's okay. He had a good life. Mom and Dad want me to try to convince Grandma to move to Portland with them. I don't think it's happening though. She loves this town."

"How long are you planning on being here?"

"I'm not sure. I took a leave of absence from work."

"What kind of work?"

"Elementary teacher."

A smile spread across his lips when he looked her way again.

"What?"

"It suits you."

"Thanks. I think," she replied with a frown, and he laughed. The warm sound made her shift on the seat, heat curling in her belly and spreading down her legs.

"You never did take compliments very well."

"When did you ever compliment me, Cade Weston? If I remember correctly, neither you nor Kale ever gave me the time of day, much less a compliment."

The lights of her grandmother's house came into view, and he pulled into the driveway, shut the truck off, and said, "Teenage boys don't know how to give compliments, Nat. You've changed since all of us were kids."

"I know, cynical and bitter."

"No, I mean you've turned into a real beauty. I certainly don't see the gangly teenage girl I remember. I'm sure we've all had issues and problems over the span of time."

"Sorry. I didn't mean to dump on you."

"It's okay. Obviously there is some sourness."

"Yeah, well, maybe I'll tell you about it someday. For now, I need to get inside. I'm sure my grandmother is worried sick. Thanks for the lift," she said, pushing open the door. "I guess I'll see you around."

"Probably. I'm always around somewhere," he replied. "Be careful going up those steps. They might be a bit icy."

"Thanks for the warning, but I do remember winters in Montana; very cold, very windy, and not much fun."

"Unless you are sledding down Marshall Hill."

"People still do that?"

"All the time."

"Man. I haven't been sledding in forever." After they moved to Oregon, rarely did her family do anything like sledding together. Her parents fought a lot since her mom hadn't wanted to leave Red Rock and her dad worked all the hours he could get to buy them a house. She shook her head to clear the melancholy thoughts.

Life got lonely for the awkward fifteen-year-old from the hick town in Montana.

Her sister, Andrea, felt the same way, although, much younger than Natalie, friends came much easier to her and fitting in hadn't been such a chore.

"Let me get your suitcase and walk you to the door," he said, opening the drivers' side.

"I can get it."

"I'm trying to be a gentleman here, Nat," he said with a smile. "My parents did raise me to be one, even if I didn't take to it very well sometimes."

Moments later, he stood at her side of the truck and held the door open for her.

When she stepped onto the driveway, her foot slipped, and she grabbed the door of the truck, Cade's arm whipping around her waist to steady her.

"Careful."

Heat spread from where his hand touched, down to her toes, and back up, settling low in her stomach. No man made her react this way, not even Steven; the man she once loved, or thought she had, for over two years before he decided he needed someone younger, prettier, and skinnier. Sure, she wasn't model thin. Her lips had a little natural pout to them, and her legs seemed somewhat long, but overall, she didn't think she was ugly or anything.

"Thanks," she whispered, looking up at his face.

Damn, he's hot. Always was, but I almost forgot about his rugged good looks. And the way he filled out with muscles and bulges in all the right places...yummy.

Her shoulder brushed his chest, and she wondered if he had lots of hair or only a little. The few times she'd seen him and Kale without shirts, they'd been young enough not to have much, but now it made her wonder.

The boys around Red Rock used to swim in the river meandering south of town, and many times, she and a few of her friends would watch from the bridge. Pre-pubescent boys had her all a twitter at fifteen, just like any girl her age. Cade and Kale were some of the cutest boys in school and *everyone* wanted their attention, including her at the time. They'd both been more into the popular girls. The cheerleader types—not the band geek, like her.

"This driveway is pretty slick."

"Grandma probably hasn't had anyone shovel it in a while. It looks like the drifts are pretty high."

"Yeah," he replied, stepping back and grasping her arm with one hand while holding her suitcase in the other. "Take small steps. It'll make it easier to walk on."

Giving him an exasperated glance, she said, "You know, it does snow in Oregon sometimes too."

His lips lifted in a grin. "But this gives me a reason to hold your arm."

Stepping onto the porch, she moved out of his reach as the light flipped on and her grandmother opened the door.

"Natalie Marie? Is that you?"

"Yes, Grandma. It's me."

"Who's with you, honey?"

"Cade Weston, Grandma. He drove me here since it's snowing so badly. I managed to put my car in a ditch outside of town."

"Well, Cade. Come on in and sit a spell where it's warm."

"I would, ma'am, but I'm on my way home. I've got a mare tryin' to foal."

"Nonsense. I'm sure you could use a cup of coffee to warm you. Now get in here. We're lettin' all the heat out."

Cade laughed, and Natalie had to smile when he said, "Yes, ma'am."

"No use arguing, you know."

"Not with your grandmother."

When they stepped inside and shut the door, Cade took off his hat and Natalie got the full affects of his devastating good looks. The jean jacket and T-shirt stretched over his chest like a second skin. Worn blue jeans hugged his lean hips, and pointed-toe cowboy boots completed the picture of the Montana cowboy to a 'T'.

The rough clearing of a throat brought her gaze back to his face as heat flushed her cheeks when she caught his gaze. His lips twitched with mirth when he tried to hold back his grin.

Busted!

"Sit. The couch is comfortable. I have coffee brewing anyway. I figured Natalie would want some when she got here."

"After you," he said, sweeping his arm aside in one of the most gallant gestures she'd ever seen.

Whoa! Wait just a damned minute here. Stop thinking he's some white knight or something — even if the thought of those rough hands and some delicious sex seems really good right now. How long has it been again? Too frickin' long! The last time with Steve even sucked and not literally.

"What have you been up to Cade?" her grandmother asked from the kitchen.

"Not much ma'am. Stayin' out of trouble, or tryin' to."

"How's your wife?"

Well, shit! So much for a hot romp with a sexy cowboy.

"What's her name again, Cade? Cindy, I think," her grandmother continued, oblivious to Natalie's disappointment.

"Uh, we divorced about four years ago, Mrs. Oliver."

Okay, maybe the hot romp with a sexy cowboy isn't out.

"Oh? I'm sorry to hear the news. Natalie never has married. Too busy taking care of other people's kids."

Blue eyes fastened on her and she shifted on the seat.

"Grandma, can we not talk about my lack of marriage please?"

"She did have a steady man for awhile, but Steve was a jerk and a liar," her grandmother told Cade. "I told you from the beginning, but you wouldn't listen to your grandmother. I'm glad you came to your senses before you got into anything permanent." The statement directed at Natalie, making her cheeks fill with heat at her grandmother's words.

A quick breath blew the hair off her forehead and she mouthed 'sorry'.

He reached over and squeezed her fingers. Electricity shot up her arm, sending delicious sensations across her nipples.

Damn it!

Her grandmother handed Cade a cup of coffee, and one to her, before taking a seat in the recliner across from the two of them.

"How long are planning on staying, Natalie?" her grandmother asked.

"I don't know. However long you need me to, Grandma. I took a leave from the school, so I can stay until whenever."

"Well, maybe Cade can take you out to dinner one night so you aren't cooped up here in this house with me all the time. There's no need for you to be here all day, every day. When you call your mother and father, tell them I am *not* moving to Oregon. I'm staying right here in Red Rock."

"Grandma, Cade doesn't have time to worry about ferrying me around town. Besides, it's not as if I'm not a native. And yes, I'll tell Mom and Dad you aren't moving to Oregon."

"Actually, I'm not busy tomorrow. I was going to offer to come over and shovel the driveway for you, Mrs. Oliver, and I'd love to take you out to dinner, Nat. You know, for old time's sake."

"See. He wants to take you out to dinner," her grandmother said with a wink.

"I appreciate the offer, Cade, but I really should spend some time with my grandmother, and I..."

"Nonsense. The handsome gentleman asked you out for dinner. You'll go if I have to push you out the door."

She tipped her head back on her shoulders and laughed. "All right, Grandma. You make it sound like I haven't had a date in forever."

"Only since your scumbag, short-dicked..."

"Grandma!"

"Okay, so I don't know whether he was actually short-dicked or not, but I *know* scumbag fits the bill."

A roar of laughter filled the air, and she glanced at Cade with a grin and a shake of her head.

Cade came to his feet and said, "I really should be getting back to the house. Thank you for the coffee, Mrs. Oliver."

Natalie stood to walk him to the door, ignoring her grandmother's wink when Cade's back turned.

"I'll be over bright and early to shovel the snow."

"It's okay. You really don't need to—"

One finger against her lips stopped her words.

"I want to. Besides, it gives me a reason to see you again."

"You asked me out to dinner, remember?"

"True. Okay, it gives me a reason to see you before five tomorrow evening."

"All right already. Be careful out there, huh?" A quick glance out the door told her the snow had slowed dramatically. "I'm sure the roads are still slick, and if the temperature drops anymore, the snow will ice over."

"I will. Don't forget, this weather is nothing new to me. I'm a born and bred Montana boy. I'll see you in the morning," he replied with a wink. "Sleep well."

She watched him walk to his truck and slide inside as the interior light illuminated his face. The headlights came on, and she could see the outline of his hand lift in a wave before backing out of the driveway and disappearing down the street.

A shiver rolled down her back, and she wasn't quite sure if it came from the look in his eyes when he put his finger against her lips or the frigid air outside.

Cade Weston. High school jock. All around hunk and he wants to take me out to dinner. Who would of thought?

Chapter Two

"You're taking who out to dinner?" Kale asked on the other end of the phone the next morning.

Cade and Kale remained best friends even after high school and through turbulent marriages on both their parts, but each came to their senses when their wives became lovers. Both women broke the news at dinner one night. They informed their husbands they'd decided they were lesbians and wanted to be together—without the men.

"Natalie Bennington. Remember her from high school?" Cade replied as he pulled on his jeans, T-shirt, and thick socks. He'd planned to be at Mrs. Oliver's first thing this morning, but the sun already started a good trek across the sky before he rolled out of bed. He'd been up half the night with the foaling mare at the barn on his property. The house wasn't complete yet, but the barn and the pasture areas were.

"Yeah, kind of geeky looking band girl. Didn't she have long blonde hair, green eyes, and braces?"

"You got it, but now she's hot! Oh my God, hot!"

"How would you know?"

"She put her car in a ditch outside of town. When I left the bar, heading home, I found her. The drive train busted and the car stopped ass end in the gully. I'm glad she didn't get hurt, but her car wasn't going anywhere, so I took her to her grandmother's."

"Playing the knight in shining armor, huh?"

"I guess, but let me tell you when I saw her face, I about shit, man. Thick hair you could really wrap your hands in, big green eyes with little flecks of gold, and legs that could stop traffic. I'm gettin' hard just thinking about her."

Kale's tolerant chuckle reverberated through the phone line. "So where has she been?"

"Her parents moved to Oregon after the plant closed."

"And she's back here now, why?"

"Remember readin' about Doc Oliver dyin' a week or so ago?"

"Yeah."

"He was her grandfather. I guess she's here to help her grandmother somehow."

"She's not staying long then."

"I don't know for sure. She said she took a leave of absence from her teachin' job."

"A teacher?"

Cade grunted in affirmation. "Elementary."

"Figures. I would have pegged her for the teacher type even way back then. Where are you taking her for dinner?"

"The Millhouse, I think."

"Wow! Going all out, aren't you?"

"I figured what the hell, you know. I haven't taken anyone on a date in months, much less been laid."

"You think she'll go for a little short term fun?"

"Maybe. She hasn't had a steady guy for a while from what her grandmother said. Mrs. Oliver made sure to tell me too."

"Figures."

"I better go, Kale. I told them I'd be over this mornin' to shovel the drive. Two women tryin' to do it didn't sit well with me."

"Okay. Call me later."

Cade hung up the phone, grabbed his truck keys, and slipped on his jacket. Within moments, he pulled in front of

Mrs. Oliver's house, noticing first thing—Natalie's car sitting on the street near the mailbox.

"Stubborn woman," he grumbled, shutting his vehicle off and popping open the door. "I would have taken her to the garage to have them tow it here."

The next thing he realized was Natalie standing in the middle of the driveway with a shovel in her hands.

"I told you I would be here, Nat."

Her hand shoved a few wisps of hair out of her face. "Oh, hi, Cade. I know you did, but when you weren't here by ten, I started without you."

"You did a good job, but let me finish it. Women shouldn't be shoveling snow."

One perfectly arched eyebrow shot up. "Excuse me? Are you going all male-chauvinistic on me?"

Oh shit!

"Sorry. I didn't mean it the way it came out. Men are built bulkier and with more muscle mass to handle physical labor better than women."

The shovel made it into a pile of snow and stood upright with a *twang*. Her eyes narrowed, and he wasn't sure if he would make it out of this alive, even if she was damned cute all flustered and pouty.

"Besides," he said, wrapping one arm around her waist and tugging her closer. "What does it hurt to let a man take care of you a little?"

Before he could change his mind, he brushed his lips over hers in a quick kiss then released her.

"Why don't you make some hot coffee? I'll have this done in a minute."

Her lips pressed into a firm, straight line, but lifted in a small smile at his wink.

"All right. Black?"

"Yeah," he replied, slipping his jacket off his shoulders, leaving him in nothing more than his T-shirt.

The shoveling would work up a sweat in no time if he left his coat on. A quick glance in her direction, gave him the enticing view of her backside in a nice pair of jeans as she made her way up the stairs.

Damn! She even has a nice ass to go along with everything else.

A honk from a car behind him drew his attention to the street. He almost groaned when he saw the familiar sight of Kale's Chevy.

"Hey bro," Kale said, stepping out of his truck.

"What are you doin' here?"

"Our conversation this morning had me wondering. I figured I'd check out Ms. Natalie myself."

"Great," he said with a groan.

Moments later, Natalie returned with coffee in hand.

"Holy hot damn," Kale whispered only loud enough for Cade to hear.

"Told you."

"Well, well, if it isn't Kale Dunn. What brings you by?" she asked, stopping next to him and handing Cade the cup.

"Cade told me this morning he ran into you and planned to come over and shovel the driveway. I thought I'd be a gentleman and help."

Cade covered his snort with a cough.

"Isn't that sweet? But I really don't think there's enough for two strong, healthy men to do. The drive isn't very big, after all."

"How about I keep you company while Cade shovels then?" Kale asked with an innocent look.

Cade felt like punching him.

"Great! Come on up to the house. I know Gram has more coffee and probably even some of her coffee cake left."

With his mouth hanging open, Cade watched Kale slip and arm around Natalie's shoulder and walk with her to the door.

"Well I'll be a son of a bitch. I'm gonna kill him," he growled under his breath.

It only took him about fifteen minutes of heavy shoveling to clear the driveway, especially after getting pissed at Kale for honing in on Natalie. True, they'd shared a woman or two over the years. Okay, maybe like ten from before they married and after their divorces, but Cade didn't have any idea if Nat would be one of them.

A one-man woman comes to mind with her, but then again, I could be wrong. Maybe she might be up for a little adventure after her lack of relationship lately.

The shovel found a spot next to the garage door before he headed up the porch. A high-pitched, tinkling laughter met his ear when he stopped at the front door. With a quick peek through the curtains, he saw Nat and Kale sitting close together on the couch with her grandmother sitting across from them. The intense uneasiness sweeping through him, didn't sit well. Possessiveness and jealousy weren't new feelings for him. They'd been the primary reaction to the news of his ex-wife's betrayal, but having them for a woman he hardly knew, had him wondering at the reasons.

He lifted his hand, rapping on the door a couple of times.

"Come on in, Cade. You don't have to knock," Natalie said, pushing open the screen. "It didn't take long to shovel the drive at all. It would have taken me a lot longer, I'm sure."

"I don't think it's supposed to snow again for a few days at least. Hopefully it'll stay clear for you for a little while anyway."

"Let me get you a refill on your coffee and you can sit a spell."

"Maybe Cade wants to go to lunch along with you and Kale, Nat. Wouldn't that be nice?" her grandmother said with a twinkle in her eye. His gaze focused on his friend, and Kale mouthed *what* as he returned the scowl.

Nat took his coffee cup into the kitchen, but called out, "I don't know, Gram."

"Nonsense, Natalie. Having two men fight over you seems like a wonderful idea, even to this old lady."

Her face flushed with color when she returned to the living room, hot coffee in hand. Cade figured he'd let her off the hook. Having lunch with her and Kale wasn't in his plans, but making tonight special for her was.

"You know, I'm sure it would be a great time having lunch with you two, but I'll have to pass. I have an appointment I can't get out of early this afternoon, but I'll be here right at five to pick you up for dinner. Sound like a plan?"

"Mmm…sure, Cade," she replied with a frown crinkling the skin between her eyebrows. "Where are we going for dinner? You know, so I know whether to wear a dress or jeans."

"It's a surprise, but wear a dress," he said. "I plan on pamperin' you tonight."

"Oh?"

"Yep." Taking the seat on the other end of the couch, he thought it amusing when she seemed uncomfortable sitting between him and Kale.

If she only knew how much I'd like to sandwich her between the two of us, in other ways.

Little Miss Natalie Bennington definitely had his interest and it appeared she also garnered Kale's. Rather funny actually, in high school, she wasn't his type or Kale's, at all. Cheerleader, blonde, built like a brick shit house, and loose panties fit the description of those making it into their favor. Natalie was the shy girl who stayed away from the football players, preferring to spend her time with the others in the band and those into the science stuff.

"You didn't say how long you planned to stay, Nat," Kale said.

"I really don't know. It depends how long Gram needs me. I don't have anything back in Oregon holding me at the moment, so I can be here for a while if need be."

"Wonderful. I'd really love to get to know the Natalie Bennington you've turned into," Kale replied, brushing his fingers against her shoulder when he put his arm across the back of the couch. Cade clamped his jaw so hard, his teeth hurt. The insane urge to snap Kale's fingers rushed through him.

A heavy sigh left her lips and Cade wondered why.

He finished his coffee and stood. "I'd better get going so I don't miss my appointment. Walk me out?" he asked, taking her hand in his.

"Sure," she replied, coming to her feet.

They walked outside, hand in hand, and he liked the feeling of her warm palm in his.

The smile on her lips and the shy way she dropped her gaze, made him feel like a kid again. Like a first date or something.

I guess it will be in a way. We never dated in school.

"You really don't have to go out of your way tonight, Cade. I know you probably feel cornered into dinner with my grandmother's suggestion and all."

He let go of her hand and wrapped an arm around her waist. "I want to, Natalie. Why can't you believe that? I find you extremely attractive, funny, cute, and I want to see what makes you tick," he whispered, brushing his lips against her ear. When he moved back, her big green eyes drew him in, making him want to feel the softness of her lips under his again. The miniscule brush of their mouths before did nothing but whet his appetite for more. He wanted to stroke the inside of her mouth and feel her return the hot brush of his tongue. He wanted to know what it felt like to have her give herself to him and let need take over.

Seconds later, his mouth hovered over hers—wanting but waiting for her to give him some indication she needed it too.

A slight shift of her weight toward him gave him the answer he sought.

The cell phone in his pocket rang, and he closed his eyes with a groan.

Damn it!

He knew that ring tone—his sister.

Impeccable timing.

"Sorry," he whispered, stepping back and pulling out his cell. "Hi, Elizabeth."

"Hey, Cade. Mom wants to know if you are coming over for lunch today."

"I planned to. Is there a problem?"

"No. She wants you to stop at the store on your way and grab a few things."

"Fine. I'll call you when I get there. Bye, sis." The phone shut with a click. "I guess I'll see you tonight."

Natalie nodded and rubbed her arms.

"I shouldn't keep you out here. It's too cold without a jacket," he said, running his hands over her bare flesh.

"I'm fine. Thanks for shoveling the driveway."

"You're welcome. Anytime." A heavy sigh rushed from between his lips. "I better go before Elizabeth calls back wondering where I am." Not wanting to walk away without feeling her lips, he brushed his mouth over hers, smiling to himself when she lifted up on her toes to meet him halfway.

* * * *

God, he tastes good. I really want more, but here and now is not the place.

"Mmm...you better go," she whispered, after a quick sweep of his lips.

"Yeah. I'll see you in a little while."

"All right. Five o'clock, right?"

He nodded and opened the door to his truck.

Moments later, he waved and pulled away from the curb, heading down the street.

When she turned toward the house, Kale stood at the door, leaning against the frame with his arms over his broad chest and a wicked smile on his lips.

How the hell did this happen? I'm having lunch with Kale and dinner with Cade. I would never have thought in a million years, I'd see either of them on this trip home, and here I am, having meals with them on the same day. This is totally unbelievable and so crazy it's funny.

As she headed toward the house, Kale opened the screen for her. "Ready for lunch?"

"Uh, sure. Let me grab my purse and we can go."

Her shoulder connected with his chest when she brushed by him, sending exciting tingles down her arm.

Whoa! Wait just a damned minute here.

A quick glance into his dark chocolate eyes and she almost forgot where she was going. The two men were such a contrast. Kale with his dark good looks, hot build, hard thighs, and trim waist, could make any woman cream her panties, and then there's Cade, all light brown hair, baby blues hot enough to melt butter, solid chest, and lips so soft, she wasn't sure he even kissed her, and man, could he kiss!

"I...um..."

"Your purse?"

The rush of air against her lips when he spoke had her wondering if his kiss would be any different than Cade's.

"Oh…uh…yeah."

Within a few minutes, he had her seated in his truck and they were driving down the now plowed street, toward town.

"So. What have you been up to since high school?" she asked, curious about the direction of his life.

"School and work. The normal stuff."

"School? You went to college somewhere?"

"Yeah. University of Montana, actually. I got a football scholarship out of high school and got my degree in Architecture."

A laugh bubbled from her lips. "You and Cade always were the stars of the team."

"Kind of hard not to be when I played quarterback and he played tight-end. Didn't you play in the band?"

"Yes, the flute."

"Ah. I remember. The shy band girl."

"I wasn't shy."

"Yeah, you were, Nat. If I even said hi to you, you'd mumble and glance away."

"Neither you or Cade knew I existed. And I'm not sure why both of you are playing with me now." Trepidation slipped down her back. *This is all a game to them. See who can get to the timid, lonely, never been married woman, first.* "You know, I think you should take me back to my grandmother's."

"What? Why?"

"I'm not going to allow you or Cade to amuse yourselves with me. I might never have married, Kale, but I know players when I see them, and you two fit into the category perfectly. I refuse to be the toy you two pull apart."

He stopped the truck on the side of the road, put it in park before he turned toward her, and captured her hand in his.

"Listen, Nat, this has nothing to do with me and Cade wanting to see who can get in your panties first."

A snort left her mouth.

"Really, I'm not." He brought her hand to his mouth and kissed her fingers. "Cade did call me this morning and tell me he rescued you last night, and that I wouldn't believe how hot you'd turned out. Truthfully, I came by because I wanted to see for myself, and I do have to say, you are one gorgeous woman. I can't understand why some lucky guy hasn't snatched you up already."

"You could have any woman you want. Why me?"

"I'm curious. I don't want anything from you, Nat, except to show you a good time. It's only lunch. If nothing else, I only want to talk to you over a nice meal."

After a few minutes of contemplating whether she could believe him or not, she finally agreed. "All right. I'll still have lunch with you, but I'm not looking for a relationship, nor am I looking for a lover."

"Or two?"

"Two? You aren't serious?" she asked, shock zipping down her back. *Two? Two men at once? Maybe he didn't mean it like that. But what if he did?*

"Just a thought, honey," he replied, the wicked grin returning to his face as he pulled the truck onto the road again.

Okay, maybe he did mean it.

When he pulled up in front of The Blue Bonnet Café, she almost laughed. The café had been the hang out for the local kids ever since she could remember. They always giggled at the "grownups" when they came in.

"What's so funny?"

"I can remember hanging out here when we were kids."

"We never hung out here."

"No. You had your little blonde cheerleader types and I had my friends."

"Well, I hope I've out grown looking at only what's on the surface."

Her shoulders lifted in a shrug.

"Come on. They still have the best burgers in town, and I'm starving."

When they headed for the door, he placed his hand at the small of her back. The warmth from his palm did nothing to help her all of the sudden, out of control libido.

This is crazy. Yeah, both of them are drop-dead gorgeous in their own way, but why am I like, ready to drool all over both of them? Why can't I be attracted to one?

"You okay?" he asked, pressing his lips against her ear briefly before she slid into the booth on one side while he took a seat on the other.

"Yeah. I'm fine. This is all a little weird for me."

"Weird how?"

The waitress stopped at the edge of their table and asked for their drink order, stopping their conversation for a moment, but the need to get this out in the open wasn't about to be forestalled. Once their coffee cups were full and each doctored it the way they liked, she said, "Come on, Kale. I'm really not your type or Cade's."

"How do you know our type hasn't changed over the years?"

Okay. I'll play. "What did Cade's wife look like?"

"You remember Cynthia Bishop?"

"Yes, well sort of."

"That's who Cade married."

"See? Blonde, pretty, big boobs."

"And lesbian."

"What? You can't be serious. Really?"

His tempting lips wrapped around the edge of the cup, and he took a healthy drink. "Yes. My wife came from Bozeman. I met her in college, and after we got married, we moved back here. The four of us spent a lot of time together. The two girls became best friends, and more, as time went on. We didn't realize they had taken their relationship into the 'lover' status until one night we were all having dinner at their place and they broke the news they wanted divorces."

"Both of them at the same time?"

"Yeah. When we tried to get out of them what the issues were, they finally confessed they'd become lovers and didn't want us in their lives anymore."

"Wow," she whispered, amazed any woman in her right mind would walk away from either him or Cade, much less for another woman.

"So you see, we've both been burned, and truthfully, I'd love to find a woman I could classify as a real woman. Not one necessarily into shopping at the high-end department stores just because she can, or needs big parties and hanging out with the *in* crowd. I want someone who likes hanging out on Saturday's with me. Maybe watching football even if she doesn't like the game, but wants to because she wants to be near me."

"I can understand your feelings."

The waitress returned for their lunch order, giving her a little time to digest what Kale said. The difficulty came with wrapping her mind around him and Cade's attraction to her. It didn't fit.

"I'll have a cheeseburger and fries, please," she told the waitress.

"The same for me."

"Great. I'll check on you two in a bit."

"Your grandmother seems to be dealing with your grandfather's death pretty well."

"It's not like she didn't know it was coming. He'd been ill for some time, but being a doctor, he wasn't about to get treatment."

"Did he have something specific that caused his death?"

"Yes. He'd been dealing with prostate cancer for a while."

"Well, I'm sorry to hear about his passing. He was a favorite around here."

"I know. It killed my mom to move to Oregon when we did. I didn't really care for it either. Being a sophomore in high school and moving really sucked."

"You must have coped pretty well."

Their food arrived, saving her from commenting on his observation. She didn't think she'd dealt well at all. Yeah, she had a few friends, but not like here in Red Rock. This was home even if it wasn't anymore.

"Did you ever think about coming back here after finishing school?"

"I had to stay there. The cost of college in Oregon played a huge part in my decision to stay, and then, afterwards, the school district close to my parents offered me a lucrative salary to teach."

"Cade said you teach elementary students," he said, popping a French fry in his mouth.

"I do and I love it. The kids are great," she replied, stirring the cream into her coffee after the waitress refilled it. "I never thought of doing anything else."

"They are lucky to have you."

Her gaze caught his, and she cocked her head to the side a little. "I don't understand you at all, Kale."

"What's there to understand?"

"Both you and Cade seem so different from what I remember. It's really hard for me to wrap my mind around it."

He grasped her fingers and squeezed. "We are both simple guys who work hard, play hooky occasionally, still ride horses, sometimes rodeo on the weekends, and hope to find the right woman someday. Nothing more. You're like a breath of fresh air around here. You know in Red Rock, people get on the bus, but they don't get off."

She couldn't help but smile since she knew it to be true for the most part. After her family moved, they did come to visit occasionally, but they never stayed long. Her dad loved Oregon and couldn't wait to get back.

Talk turned to other things like the small place he owned outside of town, some of the children she taught, and the coming Christmas season.

"What's your place like?"

"A typical cattle and horse ranch. I breed and train horses, but I also run some cattle on the property too."

"I imagine it keeps you really busy," she replied, picking at the remaining food on her plate.

"Most of the time. We should be calving and branding soon and that will take up about three weeks of non-stop work. I don't get much sleep during those times, but it's still a couple of months away. When I'm not working the cattle, I've got the horses to keep me busy. Unfortunately, the market for horses unless they are racehorses, isn't much. People aren't riding for pleasure as much these days."

"What about your family, Kale?"

"What about 'em?"

"Do they still live here?"

"Yeah. They own The Double D and are more into cattle than horses these days."

"Cade helps me out there. In fact, he has a small apartment here in town he sleeps in some nights, but for the most part, we share my place. The house on the property is big enough for a whole family with a passel of kids."

"What do you call yours?"

"The Bar KD."

"Your wife didn't take it when you divorced?" A frown scrunched the skin between his eyebrows, and she said, "I'm sorry. It's none of my business."

"Its fine, Nat. No, she didn't take it. She didn't want it. She hated the ranch and everything it stands for. I don't know why she ever agreed to marry me if she felt that way."

"I'm sorry. It must have been really hard."

"It doesn't matter. She got what she wanted, and I'm glad she's not in my life anymore." One French fry slipped between his tempting lips. "What about you? Cade said you were in a long-term relationship."

A heavy sigh left her mouth, and she traced the water droplet on her glass for a moment.

"If you don't want to talk about it, that's fine."

Her gaze caught his, and she felt a shiver roll down her back at the look in his eyes—the look of someone who cares and really wants to know.

After a quick inhale, she said, "I was with Steve for two years. We talked about getting married a time or two, but he never asked really. I never thought there were any problems, until I came home early from a teacher's conference in Seattle. I wanted to surprise him, but he surprised me when I walked into our bedroom and found him in bed—our bed, with another woman."

"I don't understand how people can cheat on each other," Kale replied, pushing his plate away. "I mean, if you don't want to be with your partner anymore, get out of the relationship and move on."

"I know. I never thought about being with someone else while I was with Steve."

"You don't seem to be the type of woman to cheat."

"How would you know, Kale?" she asked with a smile. *Mmm...he wants to know more about me, does he?*

"I don't, but I'd like to. You're a fascinating woman, Natalie Bennington, and I would love to spend more time with you while you're here."

"What about Cade?"

"What about him? You haven't even been on a date with him yet."

"No, but he asked me out first. It's kind of weird to be dating two men."

His eyes twinkled and his lips twitched with a suppressed smile, and she had to wonder what he found so funny.

"Cade and I don't compete for women."

"You don't?"

"Listen, let me take you back to your grandmother's, and we can talk more there."

Okay. Well, that's kind of strange, but whatever, I guess.

Kale paid the bill and escorted her to his truck. The ride back to her grandmother's house seemed almost uncomfortable, although, she wasn't sure why. A song came on the radio, and she hummed along with the tune of Kenny Chesney singing, 'I'd Love To Change Your Name'.

"You know this one?"

"Yeah. I like Kenny Chesney. I have a lot of his CD's."

"I like his stuff too, but George Strait is my favorite."

"Kind of hard to top 'ole King George." A warm laugh left his mouth and she smiled. "You have a nice laugh, Kale."

"Thanks."

They pulled into her grandmother's driveway, and he came around to her side to open the door. His palm appeared in front of her to help her out, and she realized how much she missed the gentlemanly behavior of the Montana cowboy.

"I appreciate you taking me out for lunch. It was very sweet of you," she said, while they walked toward the porch.

"You're welcome. We really need to talk, but I think I'll wait for a better time."

She stopped and said, "Are you sure? You seemed pretty adamant we would talk."

"Yes, I'm sure. It's kind of a weird subject and we really need to be able to discuss it."

The warmth of his hand at the small of her back made her quiver with desire, curling a knot of need in her belly.

When she turned to face him, he cupped her face between his palms and brushed his lips against hers. The softness of his lips took her by surprise, as did the feelings he stirred. Comparing his and Cade's kisses, she realized both were intoxicating in their own way.

"I'd better go even though I don't want to. I would much rather stay and kiss you, but I've got work to do at the ranch." He stepped back and stuffed his hands in his pockets, as if he wasn't sure he could keep them off her. "Can I take you out again on Saturday?"

"I don't know, Kale, I…"

He took her hand in his and brought it to his mouth. The scrape of his whiskers along the back of her hand sent shivers up her arm. Soft lips slipping across her skin's surface and the brush of his tongue made her lips part on a sigh.

"Please?"

The dark brown of his eyes mesmerized her. A small smile graced his mouth, and she heard herself agreeing.

"How about six o'clock? We can have dinner and go dancing or something."

"Six is good," she murmured.

"I'll see you then." Another brush of his lips and he was gone.

Chapter Three

The knock on the door startled her. *Is it five already?* She jumped to her feet to answer it, smoothing the skirt of her black dress with her hands. Anticipation of the coming dinner date with Cade had her on edge since Kale had dropped her off after lunch. Slick sweat irritated her palms, goose bumps flittered across her arms, and her mouth felt dry. Two hours getting ready for this date did nothing to calm her nerves. She'd tried on everything she brought with her and still couldn't find anything suitable to wear. A quick trip to one of the local boutiques yielded the perfect dress and shoes—never mind the hundred-dollar price tag.

A deep sigh left her lips as she approached the front door and opened it.

The porch light reflected the gleam of gold in Cade's hair, making it almost look like a halo around his head. Angel he wasn't, she decided. Maybe he was hiding little horns underneath because he sure knew how to make her think about hot sex between the sheets.

His black suit jacket fit across his broad shoulders like a second skin, hugging each muscle and bulge of his magnificent body. The stark white shirt made his tan skin appear almost bronze as the collar peeked above the lapels of his coat. One large hand cradled his black Stetson like a baby. Every Montana cowboy loved his cowboy hat. It came with the territory.

His baby blues dilated when they stopped on her face. "Wow," he whispered. The smile spreading across his lips made her feel beautiful and sexy in the strapless black dress she'd chosen. She knew it hugged her curves and emphasized her cleavage. For some reason, she loved the look in his eyes.

"Come in. It'll only take a minute to grab a coat and my purse."

The screen swung out, allowing him to step inside the house.

Natalie turned around only to find her grandmother standing next to the couch, a big smile on her face and a mischievous twinkle in her eye.

"You look very nice. Where are you taking Natalie for dinner?" her grandmother asked.

"It's a surprise." A beautiful bouquet of red roses was clutched tightly in his hand, almost as if loosening his grasp would cause them to disappear. "These are for you."

"Oh my. They're gorgeous, Cade. Thank you," she said, kissing him on the cheek.

His gaze dropped to the floor, and she could have sworn pink flushed his cheeks. "I wasn't sure you liked roses, but they're usually a safe bet for a woman."

"Let me run into the kitchen and put them in water. Then we can go." Quick steps took her into the other room, but she could still hear the conversation going on in the living room.

"It's nice of you to bring flowers," her grandmother said.

"Yeah, well, my parents raised me to be a gentleman and one always brings flowers on the first date," Cade answered, and Natalie smiled. *First date? It sounds like he's planning more than one.*

"Just make sure you have her home by midnight."

"Grandma," Natalie warned from where she stood in the kitchen. "I'm not sixteen."

"I'm kidding, Natalie. Lighten up." The next words had heat crawling up her chest and staining her cheeks a bright red she was sure. "Did you put some condoms in your purse?"

"She did not just say that." Natalie grumbled, pressing her hands to her cheeks.

A roar of laughter from Cade gave her the answer. Her grandmother did indeed mention condoms.

"Don't worry, Nat. I got it covered," Cade replied, making her blush even more.

"I'm going to stay here now, and you two can go out to dinner while I die of humiliation," she yelled from the kitchen.

"No you won't. I've been looking forward to this all day." Cade stopped behind her and put his hands on her shoulders. "We're only teasing, Nat."

"I'm so embarrassed."

He tugged her around to face him and framed her face with his hands. "Don't be. It's not like the thought hasn't crossed my mind from the moment I saw you." Soft, warm lips brushed hers, and she closed her eyes at the sensations ricocheting through her. "Come on. I want to treat you special tonight. Grab your purse and coat. We have reservations."

* * * *

One of the oldest buildings in Red Rock sits on the corner of Main and Smith. The huge stone and steel structure used to be the county courthouse, but now houses The Millhouse Restaurant and Hotel. Cade pulled his truck up to the front and put it into park as a valet came around the driver's side and opened the door.

"May I park this for you, sir?"

"Sure." Cade climbed out and walked to her side. Holding the door open, he extended his palm to help her.

"Wow. When did they convert this?" she asked, taking his hand. Her gaze went up the front façade of the building, amazed at the conversion. Gray stone graced the whole front of the building, and large columns held the top overhang. Huge chandeliers, dripping with crystal accents, graced the ceiling inside the restaurant, were visible through the long windows along the front. Light reflected a multitude of color through the windowpanes and onto the concrete under their feet. Rows of box hedges sat under the windows, and under the canopy of the restaurant, large planters held enormous ferns.

"A few years ago. They made it into a high-class hotel and the best restaurant in town. It's the best food around these parts," Cade replied, tucking her hand into the crook of his arm.

"And expensive too, I bet."

"Don't worry about the cost. It's my treat since I chose to bring you here."

"But—" One finger pressed against her lips, stopping her words.

"No buts," he whispered. A quick brush of his lips against hers and she lost all train of thought. He smiled when he lifted his head and led her inside. Dark red carpet, with white and gold flowers, cradled her heels when they stepped through the gold and glass doors. They stopped next to the podium, of what she assumed was the maître d, and Cade gave his name. Immediately, they received an escort to a cozy table in the corner. Old-fashioned chairs, covered in burgundy brocade with gold accents, sat pushed under the table, and she loved when Cade pulled out the chair for her.

"Thank you," she whispered.

Goose bumps rose on her arms when he brushed his lips against her ear and murmured, "Anythin' for you darlin'."

Crystal goblets and a variety of silverware reflected the lights overhead, and she wondered if she could remember what utensil went with what. The stark white tablecloth looked elegant beyond words, and the feeling of being out of place began to overwhelm her, until Cade squeezed her fingers.

"Have I told you how beautiful you look? You take my breath away."

"I appreciate the sentiment."

"It's the truth."

The waiter stopped next to their table, asking what they wanted to drink, and Cade ordered champagne.

"Trying to get me drunk so you can find out if I really do have condoms in my purse?"

His chuckle warmed her. When he brought her fingers to his lips, kissing each one before sliding his tongue over her palm, it made her want to admit her own wanton thoughts.

"I'm only trying to loosen you up a little."

"If I get any looser, I'll be sliding under the table."

"Um…interesting idea."

Shit!

She retrieved her hand and said, "Shall we decide what to eat?"

The grin on his lips widened.

Open mouth—insert foot.

"What I meant was…"

"It's, okay, Nat. Keep goin', honey. I'm likin' where this is headin'."

Unable to hide the heat in her cheeks, she dropped her gaze to the menu and clamped her mouth shut.

"The sirloin looks good. What would you like?" he asked a few moments later.

"Typical cowboy. Red meat it is."

"Can't help it. Being born and bred on a cattle ranch does that to a man."

"The steak and shrimp sounds good. I really acquired a taste for seafood living in Oregon. The salmon out there is fabulous, and when they bring king crab legs down from Alaska… Wow."

"I don't know how this place will fair in comparison."

"Shrimp is usually a pretty safe bet, even inland," she replied, laying the menu to her left.

Once the waiter had come and gone with their order, their conversation turned to things more personal.

"Kale brought up something when we were having lunch today and I wanted to ask you about it."

A frown appeared on his face and his blue eyes darkened. "Okay. Shoot."

"He said the two of you don't compete for women."

"How did that conversation come about?"

"I told him it felt weird dating both of you, and he said you two didn't compete for women."

"We don't."

"Care to explain?"

"It's not really the type of conversation I'd like to have with you when there are other ears around."

"Oh?"

"The whole thing is rather personal."

"I see," she said, even though she had no clue what he meant. She cleared her throat and took a sip from her champagne. The bubbles tickled her nose, and she had to rub it to calm the sensation. "Kale told me you married Cynthia Bishop."

"Just full of information, wasn't he."

"He also told me how things went down between your wife and his. I can't even imagine it. I'm sorry for both of you. It must have been terrible."

"It wasn't a pleasant time in my life, no. I had no clue anything was wrong. They blindsided both of us," he replied with a frown.

I wonder if he's still pining for her.

"How long were you married?"

"Five years."

"No children?"

A rueful laugh left his mouth. "She never wanted any. The thought of ruining her figure didn't sit well with her at all."

"I don't understand how a woman can not want children."

"You have to think that way. You're a teacher."

"Actually, no I don't. There are several teachers I know who don't want children of their own."

"Really?"

"Yes. They are fine teaching other people's children, but they have no desire to raise any themselves."

"What about you? Do you want children?"

"Someday, when I meet the right man, I'd love to have several. I grew up in a lonely home."

"You had your sister."

"True, but Andrea is quite a bit younger than I am. I love her. Don't get me wrong, but we didn't have the adoring sisterly bond. After we moved to Oregon, I found myself on my own a lot. My parents fought since my mother didn't want to move there in the first place."

"I'm sorry. I can't imagine growin' up in such an environment. My family has always been close, and I have several siblings to prove it."

His grin caught her by surprise and she had to laugh.

The food arrived, and the smell of seared meat made her mouth water. It had been a long time since she'd had the kind of steak you could get in Montana.

"Wow. This looks wonderful."

"I told you they have really good food." He cut into the meat on his plate, popped a piece between his full lips, and moaned in pleasure.

"Do you come here often?"

The water in his glass almost spilled when he grabbed it, washing down the meat with an unhealthy gulp and a rough cough.

"I'm sorry. I didn't mean to make you choke. Are you all right?"

"I'm fine." The words came out in a coarse whisper.

"Are you sure?"

"Yeah. Your question caught me off guard. That's all." His eyes watered and it looked like his nose might run, too.

"Why?" she asked. One small piece of steak slipped between her lips, and she fought a matching moan to his. "Lord, this is good."

"You being here seems so natural. I forget you haven't been here in a long time." He brought the napkin in his lap up to his mouth and wiped the edge of his tempting lips. "I'm actually here all the time, although not as a patron. My family supplies the beef for this place."

"Really? Wow. It must be very lucrative for your parents place then."

"Um, yeah, it is."

Their conversation came to a screeching halt when her cell phone chimed in her purse.

"I'm sorry. I need to see who is calling. It could be my grandmother."

"No problem."

She grabbed her purse from the floor and pulled out the still ringing phone. *Steven? What the hell is he calling for?*

"Somethin' wrong?"

"No. I don't think so anyway." She hit ignore and returned it to her purse.

"Maybe you should have answered it."

"It wasn't someone I care to talk to."

"Oh?"

A frustrated sigh left her lips on a sharp exhale. "It was my ex."

"Ex what?"

"Ex-boyfriend, ex-lover—just ex."

"I see. You mean short-dicked…"

Her hand came up quickly and pressed against his lips, silencing his words. He smiled against her fingers and sucked one into his mouth. Desire, hot and needy, shot down her back, stopping at her throbbing clit.

"Mmm…tastes like chicken," he murmured, releasing her fingers.

A small snort came from her mouth, and she shook her head at his attempts to flirt. *He's damned good at it, too.*

"What?"

"You."

"What about me? Oh, I know. I'm devilishly handsome and built rugged. I have gorgeous eyes. I can rope a steer, herd cattle, ride a horse, two-step with the best of 'em, and make love to you all night long."

A high-pitched laugh bubbled from her mouth as she said, "Not the least bit modest, are you?"

"For you, darlin', I'll be all those things and more." The twinkle in his eyes and the twitch of his lips told her he could and would. All she had to do was ask. The thrill of anticipation danced through her stomach setting it quivering like a thousand butterflies, loose inside. She splayed her hand across her abdomen, wishing it would calm down before she did something stupid, like sleep with him.

* * * *

Once they finished their meal, both laughing at the waiters' suggestion of dessert, Cade paid the tab and escorted her to the podium to retrieve his truck. Getting her alone quickened his pace. The thoughts of holding her next to him, kissing her pouty lips, running his fingers through her hair, and tasting her skin while running his tongue over every inch of her made his cock harden to aching proportions.

"What's the hurry, Cade?" she asked when he whipped the door open on his truck.

"I want some alone time with you," he replied, kissing the tip of her nose. "Problem with that?"

"If it means I get to kiss you again, then nope."

"Definitely, darlin'."

He closed the door behind her and turned away to adjust his cock.

Good God, I need to get between those gorgeous thighs. I haven't been this damned horny in a long time, if ever.

"You know, Kale said you stay at his place a lot," she said when he slipped inside the cab.

"Sometimes. I wouldn't say a lot. I have my own place in town, and my mom maintains my room at the house just in case I ever decide to move back home. Not like it would ever happen. I kind of like my bachelor life."

The lights of town zipped past the windows, the cars thinning out the further they drove. *My apartment in town is nothing more than a bed, a dresser, a couch, and a television. I can't take her there.* He slept there when he did jobs in Red Rock. The other profession under his belt consisted of construction, but building slowed in the winter, leaving him more and more time to work on the home he started on his own property. For some reason, he wanted to show her his space.

"Where are we going?"

"Someplace special," he said, grasping her hand in his. "It's a little ways outside of town though. Do you mind?"

Her eyes twinkled in the lights from the dashboard and she smiled softly. "Not at all. I love that you want to show me something so meaningful to you."

"You're a special woman, Natalie." She frowned, and he wondered why when she stared out the window. "Did I say something wrong?"

When she turned toward him, he could see pain and mistrust in her eyes.

Someone hurt her badly, and right now, I could kill him. He shook his head, staring out the windshield again. *Whoa! Wait just a damned minute here. What the hell am I thinking? The last thing I need is another permanent fixture in my life. A quick romp...yes, but someone stable...no.*

"What are you thinking?" she asked in a mere whisper.

"Me?"

"Yes. You look angry."

"Well, from the look in your eyes, I'd say this ex of yours did a lot of damage."

"How so?"

"You have a wary, distrustful look, but I aim to change your opinion of men. We aren't all like your ex."

They pulled off the road and took a dirt path back several hundred yards until they came upon his partially finished house.

"Wow. Is this yours? You're building it?"

"Yeah. I do construction during the summers, and since it's slow right now, I'm working on this place. Would you like to see? It's not much right now. Just four walls, a roof, and bare studs on the inside, but it's all mine."

"I'd love to."

She reached for the door, but he stilled her hand with his own. "Let me get it."

The soft smile lighting her face did wonderful things to his insides. He moved around the back of the truck, grabbed the flashlight from the large toolbox, and then opened her door.

"We have light."

"A good thing to have out here, in the middle of nowhere, in the pitch darkness," she said. The little giggle to her voice turned to a peal of laughter when he scooped her up in his arms and walked toward the house.

"Put me down."

"Nope. I kind of like holding you, and I don't want you to freeze those pretty little toes."

The wind rustled the branches on the trees overhead and snow flurries fell in a thin veil of white. Once he reached the porch, he let her slide down his body, watching her pupils dilate, and her lips part in invitation. He wasn't sure if he could deny himself, or her, when she leaned toward him. After a mental kick, he pulled the collar of her coat up around her ears, and kissed her nose before taking her hand, entwining their fingers.

"I love the snow. It's one of the things I missed about Montana. It doesn't really snow much in Oregon."

"How about we go sledding on Marshall Hill tomorrow?"

Her face lit up like a Christmas tree. "Really?"

Laughter filled the small grove where the house was built, as they stepped up to the door. "Yes, really."

"You don't have to work tomorrow?"

"I can make time for you, Nat."

"I don't want you to get into trouble or anything, Cade. I mean, it's not that important."

The green of her eyes almost glowed with excitement at the thought of a simple thing like sledding, and he wasn't about to disappoint her. "We'll go and I won't take no for an answer. Now, let me show you my house."

They stepped inside, the smell of pine mixed with caulking, paint, glue and other construction scents, met his nose. She brushed the snow from her coat and looked around even though it was difficult to see.

"Hang on. I have a small generator on the back porch. Let me crank it up and we'll get a little more light and maybe some heat."

"I could do heat," she said, running her hands up and down her arms.

I could make you warm all over.

He cleared his throat and ducked through the doorway, ignoring the tightening pressure in his groin. She looked too damned cute standing there with her red nose and cold lips, and he wanted nothing more than to warm her in more ways than one.

Two pulls on the generator and it cranked to life. The lamps he left inside the living room came on and spread a glow throughout the room.

"Wow. This is great, Cade," she called from inside. "It's going to be really big."

"Not too big, but enough for a family anyway," he replied, returning to her side. "This is the livin' room, and there's gonna to be a river rock fireplace along the wall over there. Large picture windows will be right here so we can look out over the pasture and watch the horses and cows grazin' in the distance."

"I can picture it. It'll be beautiful," she whispered, and he wondered at the longing in her voice.

Grasping her hand, he led her to where the kitchen would be. "This is the dinin' room, and the kitchen will be against this wall with a window over the sink lookin' outside so you can watch the kids in the backyard. We'll have a huge farm table so all the extended family can visit for Sunday dinner."

She stepped in front of him and slid her hands inside his coat and around to his back. "It'll be the perfect family home." Her warm breath skimmed over the exposed area of his neck, sending chills down his back. The softness of her lips brushed against the underside of his jaw, and he fought a moan rumbling in his chest.

"Natalie," he whispered.

"Mmm."

"Nat, darlin', we'd freeze to death in here if we so much as…"

"Kiss me, Cade."

He took her face between his palms, and brushed his lips against hers. A soft little moan escaped her mouth, only to be caught by his when he fit their lips together and his tongue swept inside. Their bodies molded like one piece of a puzzle to another. One hand slipped into her hair, tangling in the long strands while the other wrapped around her back, pulling her closer. There would be no mistaking the long, thick erection pressing against her stomach. He ravished her mouth. Stroking, licking, sucking motions had her whimpering in need as her tongue met him touch for touch. The desire to feel her skin outweighed everything inside him, screaming *stop, before this goes too far*. Two fingers unbuttoned the front of her coat. He parted the material and tugged her back in. Breasts pressed flat to his chest. The silky material of her dress did nothing to hide the hard nipples poking him.

Hot and insistent desire sprang to life. Something he hadn't felt in a long time made him pull his mouth from hers and skim over her cheek to her ear.

"God, I want you," he whispered. Her answer came out in a needy whimper. Small nibbles to her ear and the whimper grew. Her coat became a vice as he pushed it off her shoulders, trapping her arms against her body with it. A lick to the spot on her neck, just under her earlobe, and her breathing hitched up a notch. Sensations rushed all his nerve endings, and he groaned as he fought the headlong dash of need to push her to the plywood floor and bury himself inside her sweet heat. He brushed a kiss over her bare shoulder and pulled her coat back into place. Green eyes blinked in confusion. Pouty lips begged him to kiss her again, but he refused to give into unyielding desire in nothing more than a fuck-fest.

"Why did you stop?"

"Because, I don't want to make love to you on a plywood floor. I want you in my bed, not here. You deserve so much more."

She laid her head on his shoulder and buried her nose in his neck. A heavy sigh rushed from her lips. The sweet floral scent of her perfume made him dizzy with desire. Heat scorched him where they touched.

"Take me home with you, Cade," she murmured. Her warm breath singed his skin and tattooed her image on his brain until he couldn't think.

"Wait right here." He quickly returned to the generator, cutting the power to the house. When he returned to the spot he'd left her, she held out her arms, and he scooped her up, holding her close to his chest.

Within moments, he had her inside his truck, speeding down the dirt road toward the highway to town.

I can't take her back to my place. It's not the spot I want to make love to her for the first time. Two fingers scratched his jaw. *But where? Kale's? No. I don't want to share her. Back to the Millhouse? I could get a real nice room there, but man! It seems so cheap doin' that.*

"Cade?" Her soft voice brought him out of his musings to see her wide green eyes staring at him from across the cab of his truck. "You're thinking too much." She unbuckled her belt and slid to the middle of the bench-seat before re-hooking her seatbelt and placing her hand on his thigh. His dick jumped in his pants. A sexy smile played on her lips, and he wondered if she knew exactly what she did to him with her touch. "It doesn't matter where we go... except, not to my grandmother's."

A nervous laugh left his mouth. "I wouldn't even think of goin' there, darlin'. Somehow, I think privacy isn't on your grandmother's agenda, although she sure seems to want us together."

"Don't get your drawers in a bunch, cowboy, she wants me with anyone who doesn't use, abuse, drink, smoke, do drugs..."

"In other words, a nice guy?"

"Yeah. A nice guy. Are there any of those around anymore?"

"I'm one."

"I know and it terrifies me."

"Why?"

"The few nice guys I've been with, I get bored. You know, they say women always go for the bad boy."

"I can be bad too," he admitted with a grin.

A little smile played on her lips, and he wanted to kiss her so bad, he could taste her on his tongue.

"I'm sure you can. After all, you did steal a car when you were younger."

"Damn. I shouldn't have told you, but if it makes me bad enough to get you, then I'm okay with it."

The next thing he realized, they reached her grandmother's street. His heart dropped in his chest when they rounded the corner and a sea of flashing red and blue lights greeted them.

"Grandma?" she whispered, terror clear in her voice.

"Easy, Nat. Let's find out what's going on."

He stopped at the curb and put the truck into park. An ambulance stood nearby and a police car was parked in the driveway. The door opened with a flick of his wrist, and he rushed around her side to help her out so he could be the rock she might need to lean on, depending on what was going on inside the house.

With one arm around her shoulders and the other holding her hand, they headed for the door, but the police officer guarding the entrance refused to let them in.

"Can I help you?" the officer asked.

"I'm her granddaughter. What's going on with my grandmother?" Natalie asked.

"The paramedics are working on her now. I'm not sure what happened. We got a call, but the caller was difficult to understand."

"I need to go inside."

"Of course," the officer replied, tipping his hat. "Cade."

"Arnie."

"You with her?"

"Yeah."

"Go on in. I'm sure they'll need some information or something."

Chapter Four

"Grandma? What's happening? What's wrong?" Natalie asked, rushing to the side of the gurney.

"I'm fine, honey. Don't worry," her grandmother said, although the words seemed slurred. Her usually bright and cheerful eyes appeared dull and the left one didn't look quite right.

Natalie squeezed her fingers, and the paramedics finished strapping her in.

"We're taking her to Red Rock hospital, if you'd like to follow," one of the paramedics told her and Cade.

"We'll be right behind you," he answered. "Why don't you change real fast, darlin'. I'm sure it's gonna be a long night, and you probably don't want to be hangin' out at the hospital in your dress."

"Is she going to be all right?" she questioned, worry knotting her stomach.

"I don't know, but we'll be there for her no matter what. Now, go on and get changed."

She watched momentarily while they wheeled her grandmother out the door before she rushed upstairs.

T-shirt and jeans. Tennis shoes. Socks. The list of clothing items rattled off in her head when she reached her bedroom and unzipped her dress, flung off her shoes, and ripped the nylons down her legs. *She'll be fine. She has to be. I don't know what I'd do without her.*

When she finally finished dressing, except for her shoes, she headed down the stairs to find Cade pacing the living room like a caged lion—a beautiful, sexy, mountain lion or something. His hands stuffed in his pants pockets, chewing his bottom lip with his teeth.

He's worried about her, too. Gotta love a man who cares about elders.

"Let me get my shoes on and we can go," she said, taking a seat on the couch.

"We'll have to take it easy. It's starting to snow again."

Her gaze ran over him from the tip of his cowboy hat to the pointed-toe boots on his feet. *He really is one of the good guys...with a little bad streak.* She stood, tugging at the bunched up material near her hips for a moment, liking the way his eyes narrowed while watching her.

"Let's go see what's wrong with Grandma," she said, taking his hand and leading him toward the door.

It's a good thing the hospital wasn't far. He had them there within fifteen minutes.

"What do you mean I can't see her?" she demanded.

The clerk behind the desk popped her gum and tapped on the keyboard. "She's being examined, and they won't let you back there right this minute. Take a seat. They'll come get you when you can see her."

"This is ridiculous. That's my grandmother back there."

"I understand. Let me see if I can get one of the nurses to come out and talk to you."

"Easy, Nat. Getting upset isn't goin' to get you anywhere in here," Cade said, pulling her tight against his side.

"I know. I just wish I knew *something.*"

He led her to a couple of chairs in the corner and forced her down on one. "I'll be right back. I'm goin' to find the vendin' machine and get us both some coffee."

"Cade?"

"Yeah?"

"Thanks for being here. I don't know how I would handle this without you."

Warm lips brushed against hers and she sighed. "Anytime, darlin'."

When he walked away, she couldn't help but notice the looks he got from the other women sitting around the waiting room, and she felt a ping of jealousy zip through her.

Jealous? I don't have any reason to be jealous. He's being a friend, nothing more.

"Never mind the way he kissed me earlier," she murmured out loud. "And what about telling him to take me home with him?"

One quick exhale blew the hair off her forehead, and she rubbed her hands up and down her arms.

This is stupid. Getting involved with him is stupid and silly, but ohmigod can the man kiss.

"Get your mind out from between your legs, Natalie. You're grandmother needed you, and you were out getting frisky with Cade Weston."

"Nat?" a familiar voice said from the doorway.

"Kale? What are you doing here?" Her gaze fixed on his familiar chiseled features and the worry in his eyes. He took a seat next to her, taking her hand between his.

"I heard your grandmother's address on the scanner at the house. I went by there, but everyone had left. Her neighbor said they took her away in an ambulance, so here I am. Are you okay?"

"I'm fine, but Gram isn't. I'm not sure yet what the trouble is. They won't let me back there." Accepting his firm reassurance, she leaned into his embrace, absorbing his strength. "I'm so scared."

"It'll be fine, honey. Don't worry," he whispered before he kissed the top of her head.

"What are you doing here?" The growl in Cade's voice took her by surprise.

"Cade," Kale said with an answering grumble.

"Kale."

"Stop it you two," she demanded, moving away from both of them. "We aren't here to start getting possessive. And I'm not going to come between you and your friendship. You two have been friends far too long."

"You aren't," Kale insisted, but she saw the narrowing of Cade's eyes.

"Here's your coffee, Nat. I brought cream and sugar since I wasn't sure how you took yours."

"I appreciate it, Cade. Thanks. I'm sure it's going to be a very long night."

"I'll be right here with you, darlin'. You know that, right?"

"You don't need to stay. I can get a cab home and—"

Two of his fingers pressed to her lips, stopping her words. "I'm stayin'."

She nodded, took his fingers, and entwined them with her own.

"You don't need to stick around, Kale," Cade said.

"What if I want to?"

"Damn it! This is nuts. Knock it off! You aren't going to pull me apart like two dogs fighting over a piece of meat."

"Miss Bennington?" the nurse called from the doorway.

"Yes?"

"You can come back now."

"Thanks." She handed her cup to Cade and said, "You two play nice."

* * * *

"What the hell are you doing here, Kale? Really?" Cade asked, resisting the urge to punch his friend. Stumbling on Kale holding Natalie when he returned with the coffee, threw him for a loop. The feelings rushing headlong across his heart seemed strange, and he wasn't sure he liked it at all.

"I told her and I'll tell you too. I heard her grandmother's address on the scanner, and I got worried. No one was at the house so I came here. I didn't realize you two were still together and you'd be here with her."

"Where else would I be? I had a date with her, remember?"

"I know. I figured you'd have gone home by now. It's going on midnight."

"What? She turns into a pumpkin at midnight?"

Kale ran his fingers through his hair, Cade almost laughed at the hairs sticking up in several directions. "Hell, I don't know. I wasn't sure if you and she might be..."

"Doin' the horizontal mambo?"

"Maybe. Shit, Cade. I know I wouldn't mind gettin' between those thighs, and I know you feel the same way."

"Watch how you're talkin' about Nat."

"You sound almost protective, there buddy. What's up? Yesterday you were all for getting her in the sack and sharing her. Now you're not?"

Right now, he wasn't sure what he felt, but the feelings she stirred out at his house and the protectiveness running rampant through his chest, made him uneasy. "I'm sorry, Kale. I don't know how I feel right now, other than if she needs me, I'll be there for her. She doesn't have anyone here. Her grandmother is her only family, and she doesn't have any friends around these parts anymore."

"You goin' out with her again?"

"Why?"

"I asked her out for next Saturday."

"And?"

"She said yes."

Jealousy reared its ugly head, sending anger and irritation down his back. "I planned on taking her sleddin' tomorrow. She said she hadn't been in a long time."

"Sounds like fun. A little snow, some hot coffee, a little snugglin' by the fire."

"That's the plan," he replied.

"You jealous she said yes to dinner with me, Cade?"

He sipped his coffee and narrowed his gaze on his long time friend. Damn right he was jealous and he didn't like it one bit. Neither of them had ever been attached to the women they shared. It always came with an unwritten law—no deep involvement—just sex. *But Natalie's different.*

"Are you?" Kale repeated. "Because, you know, we had an agreement. No involvement—"

"I know what the damned agreement is, Kale."

"You've fallen for her, haven't you? Already. Head over heels—"

"Shut up, Kale. Just shut up."

"Cade?" Natalie's voice came from a small door to his right.

He put his coffee down on the table and faced her. "What's up, Nat? How is she?"

"They think she'll be okay, but she's had a stroke. Her speech is still slurred a little and her right arm is weak, but she'll survive. She's going to need rehabilitation, and they are going to keep her tonight for observation."

Her eyes sparkled with unshed tears, and he knew she held her emotions in check. *Such a strong woman.*

"Come here, darlin'," he said, opening his arms.

A small, choked sob broke from her lips as she threw herself into his embrace, burying her face against his chest.

"Sshh. Everythin' will be okay. You'll see."

She tipped her back and said, "But what if she never recovers? She won't be able to live by herself anymore.

She'll have to go to a nursing home or something. That would kill her, Cade."

"I know," he whispered, brushing the tears from her cheeks. "We'll take it one day at a time. No use gettin' all upset about it right now."

"I thank God, I was here already. What would happen if none of us were around? Yes, she called 911 herself, but at least I'm here to help her recover." A gasp left her lips, and she stepped out of his embrace. "I have to call my parents. They are going to have a fit over this." Her steps took her back and forth in front of the door, and the thumbnail on her right hand disappeared between her lips. "If they find out I wasn't there, my mother will have a cow! I'm supposed to be here helping her and taking care of her, not out on dates with the local bad boys. Crap!"

"Natalie, listen," Kale said, coming to her side. "Your grandmother insisted you go out and have a good time."

"That's right, darlin', she did, and she would have been upset if you stayed at the house," Cade added.

Her hand waved in front of her face, dismissing the arguments they made. "It doesn't matter. My mother will *not* understand."

Cade took her hand and drew her back into his arms. "Listen, you are entitled to have a life too. She can't fault you for it anymore than anyone else."

Both arms went around his waist, and she snuggled up to him. "Thanks. You two are the best friends a girl could have." After a quick hug, she released him and said, "Do you want to come back and see her? You too, Kale. I know she's worried about me, so it will help alleviate her uncertainties if she knows you are both taking care of me."

"If it's all right, I'd like to. I want her to know she doesn't have to worry about you," he replied.

"I'm sure she'd love to see you," Nat said. "Come on."

She took one of his hands and one of Kale's and led them through the doors. The three of them walked hand in hand until they reached one corner of the emergency room. A curtained off area stood to their left, and Natalie called out to her grandmother to make sure they could come in.

"Come on in, honey. I'm decent, well if you call these damned gowns with no back so your ass hangs out for everyone to see, decent."

He couldn't help but smile. Mrs. Oliver's a feisty old bird and nothing would keep her down. "How are you feeling?"

"Like shit. You?"

He shook his head and laughed. "Nothin's gonna keep you down, is it, Mrs. Oliver?"

"Nope. Been around too damned long to let it. Old Doc, God rest his soul, always said, 'There are two theories about arguing with a woman, neither one of them works.' Now, did you two have a good time at dinner? And when did you pick up your other hunk?" her grandmother asked when she noticed Kale standing behind them.

"Grandma, don't worry about how my date went and so you know, Kale came to the hospital when he heard your address on his scanner. He was worried is all." Natalie tucked the sheet under the edge of her until her grandmother swatted at her hands. "You'll have to stay here overnight, the doctor said, so they can watch you for a bit."

"Damn it, Natalie, stop mothering me. I'm a grown woman, and I can take care of myself. And don't be calling your mother and telling her about this. She'll end up flying her ass up here and then I'll have to deal with her too. The wet behind the ears doctor already told me I needed to stay."

"Wet behind the ears, huh?" the very nice looking doctor said as he stepped up next to the bed and smiled.

"Well, yes. You can't be much older than Natalie there is, and she's my granddaughter. How old are you anyway? You married?"

"Grandma! Will you stop trying to play matchmaker for me with every man in Red Rock!"

"I love you, Nat, and I want to see you happy. Besides, I'd love it if you settled down with some nice man here." Her grandmother looked at the doctor again and asked for a second time, "Are you married?"

"Yes, Mrs. Oliver, I am, happily married," the doctor replied, twirling his wedding ring on his left hand.

"Well damn," she grumbled and Cade had to laugh. "You and Kale aren't, young man, so don't be laughing too hard. I'll have you hitched to Nat in no time if you give me half a chance."

"Do you have a gag around here somewhere," Natalie said.

Her grandmother's eyes narrowed. "Have you talked to your mother yet?"

"No, Gram."

"Then don't."

"You know I have to call them and let them know what's happened."

"No you do not, Natalie. They'll just worry and everything is fine. I'm a little weak, but with a little rehabilitation, I'll be like new."

Cade saw Natalie glance at the doctor, and he shook his head. A deep sigh left her lips, and she sat down next to her grandmother. "Gram, listen, I have no doubt with your stubborn nature, you'll do wonderful in rehab, but you have to be ready if you don't regain your strength. What happens then? You won't be able to stay—"

"Don't you dare tell me I'll have to move out of my home. Your grandfather built our house with his bare hands, to raise our children in, and I will be there until the day I die. If I have to hire someone to come in and stay with me, then I will."

"I'll stay with you, Gram. You know that."

"I appreciate the sentiment, Natalie, but you have a life too. You have the children you teach. You can't leave them in a lurch."

"I'm staying and I don't want to hear anymore about it. However long you need me, I'll be here."

Cade liked the sound of that.

A nurse strolled in a few moments later and said, "We'll be taking her upstairs to her room now."

"You go on, honey, and have your men take you on home. There's nothing more you can do here. I'm going to be tucked in and sleep for the rest of the night."

"All right, Gram. I'll come back first thing in the morning to see what they've decided and we'll go from there." She leaned over and kissed her grandmother on the cheek. "Behave yourself, please."

"We have ways of making her behave," the nurse said with a chuckle.

"Don't go getting carried away with the drugs. I don't take anything more than Tylenol for a headache now and then," her grandmother snapped. "Keep them sedatives in your pocket."

"Yes ma'am."

Once the nurse wheeled her grandmother away, Cade took her hand in his and kissed her palm. "Let's get you home and tucked in."

"Thanks Cade. You too, Kale. You've both been lifesavers for me, and I can't thank you enough."

"You're welcome, Nat," Kale replied. "We know you're kind of alone here, even though this is your home away from home."

"You have no idea."

* * * *

The three of them walked out through the waiting room hand-in-hand. Surprised looks and blatant stares followed them out the door. The hostile glances made Natalie shiver.

"Wow. Can we say uncomfortable?"

"Don't worry about those people. They don't know what's goin' on with the three of us, and they're being rude," Cade replied. "It's none of their business, and I personally don't care what people think."

"Me either," Kale added. "I'm going on home. Cade will make sure you get back to your grandmother's safe and sound. I'll check with you later on this week about our date Saturday. Okay?"

"Gosh, Kale. With everything going on, maybe we should rain check?"

"We'll see, honey. No worries."

"Thanks."

"Of course," he said, brushing his lips against hers. "I'll call you in a day or two."

Cade's eyes narrowed into agitated slits and a frown pulled down the corners of his lips.

The two of them had been snapping at each other when they were in the waiting room and she didn't like it. Jealousy came as a hard pill to swallow, and she didn't want to come between two friends.

Silence enveloped her and Cade once they settled into the cab of his truck and headed back to her grandmothers. She'd been all ready to let him take her home to get down and dirty. Now, she wasn't sure what she wanted. Oh, she wanted Cade. No doubt about it, but could she have nothing more than a short-term, quick roll in the hay? It would be so unlike the Natalie anyone knew. Her family wouldn't believe it. Her friends would think she lied because it wasn't the Natalie they know.

A short time later, Cade pulled into her grandmother's driveway, turned off his truck, and came around to her side to hold the door.

"Such a gentleman."

The sexy grin he gave her sent tingles down her arms as he pulled her close and escorted her toward the front.

She fished the key out of her purse, slipped it into the keyhole and opened the door. Paper, plastic, and miscellaneous other objects lay scattered about the living room from when the paramedics work on her grandmother. "What a mess."

"I'll help you pick up. It shouldn't take long. There really isn't too much here."

"You don't have to do—"

The brush of his warm lips over hers stopped her words.

"I want to."

Ten minutes later, the living room was spotless again, and she gave him a silly grin.

"I know it's getting late."

"Yeah, I should probably go," he replied, tucking a curl behind her ear. "I enjoyed spendin' time with you. Thank you for going out to the house with me."

"I loved it, Cade. Thanks for showing me. It'll be beautiful when you're finished."

"I guess our sleddin' date tomorrow is out of the question, huh?"

She nodded and said, "Yeah. I need to be at the hospital first thing so I can find out what the plan is for Gram."

"I'll tell you what. After we get things settled with your grandmother, we'll go sleddin'. It's less crowded around noon anyway." He took her hand and pulled her down on the couch with him. "I need to tell you somethin', Nat."

"You look so serious. It can't be that bad."

His hand slid into her hair, tugging her closer. The brush of his lips against her cheek made her sigh and close her eyes.

"I want to make love to you, Natalie." The feel of his tongue on her earlobe sent shivers down her spine. Tiny nibbles on the soft skin below her ear made her squirm on the couch. His two strong arms wrapped around her, pulling her onto his lap. His thumb brushed over her nipple and she felt it tighten into an aching bundle of nerves. He continued his trek down her neck with his lips as he unbuttoned the front of her blouse and pushed it aside. "Tell me you want this."

"Oh God yes. It's been way too long."

He lifted his head, and stared into her eyes. The blue of his gaze bore into hers while his hands cupped her face. "You're beautiful."

Unable to continue to look at the intensity of his stare, she dropped hers to his lips. Sensual, full, and delicious, she wanted them on her body. Everywhere.

"Kiss me."

"Oh, I plan to, darlin'." He kissed her eyelids. "Here." He kissed her cheeks. "Here." He kissed her nose. "And especially here." His tongue swept across the seam of her lips, coaxing her to open for him. The moan coming from her mouth didn't sound like anything she'd ever heard before—part animalistic and part inhuman, the sound took her by surprise. "You taste good. I could eat you up."

One hand palmed her breast and teased the nipple through her bra. With a quick flick of his fingers, the material parted, and the ache intensified with the look in his eyes. Hunger, raw desire, and need sparkled in the blue depths.

He closed his lips over her nipple, sucking it deep into his mouth.

Her back arched and yearning rushed through her. Red-hot longing spiraled from his suckling straight to her clit. She wanted this man—needed him with everything inside of her.

"Cade, please," she whimpered, threading her fingers in his hair.

"Where's your room?" he asked after lifting his head.

"Up the stairs and to the right. First door."

With a powerful flex of his muscled thighs, he lifted her high in the air and cradled her against his chest. Swift steps took them upstairs and to her temporary bedroom. A small lamp on the bedside table gave her just enough light to see the wicked smile on his lips and the shine of desire in his gaze. He dropped her legs, sliding her down his body. Every rock hard inch of his tempting flesh skimmed over hers. Nipples tightened and ached as they scraped over the material of his dress shirt and jacket.

"You're still dressed," she murmured. Her lips met his whiskered jaw and slipped over the surface. Her tongue circled his ear, her teeth nipping at his earlobe.

"Why, yes I am. We'll have to rectify the situation quickly." One hearty moan spilled from his lips. "If you don't knock it off, this is gonna be a short ride, darlin'. It's been a while."

"We don't want that, now do we?"

"Hell no. I want to love you slow."

"Sounds like a plan to me. By the way? You talk too much."

"You won't hear another peep out of me."

A challenge? I like challenges.

"No?"

He shook his head, and she cocked an eyebrow, letting a wicked grin play across her mouth. The slow unbuttoning of his shirt didn't garner a sound—pushing it and his jacket off his shoulders...nothing.

Oh, I don't think so.

Unbuckling his belt while her teeth nipped at his pecs and grazed his nipples, got her no response, and she smiled.

It's on baby!

His pants and boxers fell to the floor with a slight nudge of her hands. The full length of his cock sprang free, standing tall and proud against his stomach, just begging for her touch—her mouth. A quick peek through her lashes revealed his clenched jaw, the firm line of his lips as he fought the sounds in his throat, blue eyes sparkling like sunlight on the open ocean.

"Do you want to say something?"

The jerking shake of his head gave her the answer.

His fists clenched at his sides. Touching her would give him away, she knew.

She flattened her palm on his chest, slowly sliding it over the valleys and planes of his body. Goose bumps followed the path of her hand, while crisp chest hair tickled her skin. Saliva pooled in her mouth with the need to taste him. Every tempting piece of flesh called her name, urging her to bring her mouth closer still. The path of her lips followed the trail of hair from the center of his chest, across his washboard abs, to the tip of his cock. Pre-cum glistened on the slit. His breathing sounded short and raspy. She dropped to her knees, grasped both of his ass cheeks in her hands, pulling him closer. Musky male, mixed with his arousal, met her nose. She licked her lips, opened her mouth, and took the head of his cock between her lips. The swirl of her tongue around him got the desired response. A hearty moan spilled from between his lips, and he threaded his fingers through her hair.

"God, Nat," he growled.

"Mmm," she hummed against his flesh. His hips rocked toward her, taking up the rhythm of her mouth.

Several shaky breaths later, he said, "Natalie, honey, I don't wanna come in your mouth." He pulled her up in front of him and crushed his lips over hers. His tongue swept inside, tangling with hers in a dance older than time. When he freed his feet of his jeans, he walked her backward toward the bed. The edge hit the back of her knees, and he followed her down in a tangle of arms and legs. Raspy breaths flittered across her cheek and then to her ear.

"You make me crazy."

"Cade, please. I need you to make love to me."

"Oh, I will."

"Now."

"Nope. My turn to play."

Before she knew exactly what he meant, the warmth of his lips slipped down her neck and latched onto her breast. Uncontrollable desire rushed through her. Want for this man. Need for him to make her his, even if it was only for tonight. The rough calluses on his palm chafed her skin when he slid it over her belly. The sensation drove her crazy. His hand nudged her thighs apart. The material of her jeans kept them from skin-to-skin contact, but the pressure of his touch through the barrier of material had her groaning low in her throat.

"We need to get rid of these. I want to feel your skin."

The snap gave way to the insistence of his fingers, and she lifted her hips. He grasped her pants, tugging them down and off her feet. Her silky little thong did nothing to hide anything from his intense gaze.

"These are so sexy," he whispered with his lips against her belly. One finger slipped down the edge of her underwear, between her thighs, and to her pussy. The whimper trapped in her throat escaped on a sigh. Her legs parted and he chuckled softly.

"Do you want me to touch you?"

"Please," she moaned.

"Where, darlin'?"

"My…um…"

"Tell me, honey. I don't know what feels good for you." He moved to between her thighs, and she could feel his warm breath on her pussy. His tongue wet the silky material still guarding her from his touch.

Breath hitched and legs trembled.

"Here?" he asked, sliding two fingers under the elastic.

Talking became impossible. Thoughts fled, except for knowing he now lay between her thighs, and his breath felt heavenly against her goose bumped flesh.

Not waiting for her answer, he stood up, grabbed the edges of her underwear, and slipped them off. Seconds later, the moist pad of his tongue returned.

"Ah God, Cade!"

"Easy, honey," he coaxed.

In none of her previous relationships had her partner done this. Granted, she hadn't been in many. She hadn't lost her virginity until she went to college, and the guys there didn't care. It was all about them and their needs.

Slick and wet. That's what she felt when he licked from slit to clit. A moment later, he stiffened his tongue and toggled her clit.

"So sweet."

Two fingers slid into her pussy, and she thought she'd die. Her whole body tingled. He drove those tempting digits in and out, in and out, sending her to the brink and pushing her over when he flicked her clit with his tongue at the same time.

A hearty moan spilled from her lips when her climax exploded through her belly.

"Cade," she whimpered.

One…two swipes of his tongue and he kissed his way back up her abdomen. Her trembling eased, and she opened her eyes mere slits. The wicked grin on his face made her shake her head.

"What?" he asked.

"You."

"Me? I only did what I thought you wanted, although, you never really said for sure." He looked almost unsure. "You didn't like it?"

"Of course, I did. How can a woman not like that?"

"Just checkin'," he murmured against her lips.

Wanting to feel his tongue deep inside her mouth, she opened for him and moaned when he slipped it inside along hers.

The rock hard length of his erection nudged against her pussy.

He lifted his head and said, "Hold that thought. I need to grab something."

Within seconds, he returned with a condom between his fingers.

"Anticipating?"

"Hopeful."

Her gaze dropped to his chest, and she fiddled with the hair there.

"Nat? You're okay with this, right?"

When she didn't lift her eyes back to his, he put a finger under her chin.

"I…mmm. I don't want you to get the impression I do this all the time. I've only ever been with three men my entire life and—"

The kiss he placed on her lips stopped her words. The brush of his tongue against her lips forced a groan from her mouth. After a few moments of heart-stopping kissing, he lifted his head again.

"Darlin', I don't care how many men you've been with, and no, just because you are willin' to let me love you, doesn't mean I think you're loose. I'm thrilled we're here right now. I've wanted to get you like this since I helped you out of your car out there on the road. Whatever happens after this, we'll take one day at a time."

Her heart lightened with his words. This meant something to him. It had to. How could he love her like this if it didn't?

He tore the condom open with his teeth and rolled it over his impressive erection.

"Open for me, honey."

Both legs went around his waist and he eased inside her pussy.

"You feel like heaven."

She hissed between her teeth.

"Are you all right? I'm not hurtin' you, am I?"

"No. It stings a little. It's been a long time."

"I'll go slow," he whispered. "Even if it kills me."

A soft laugh left her lips. "It's okay now. Fill me up."

The tortured groans spilling from his lips made her smile as he rocked his hips, sliding all the way in. In and out. Torturously slow.

"Cade?"

"Mmm?"

"Faster. Harder."

"Ah hell, darlin'."

His rhythm increased ten-fold. Flesh against flesh. Hot, sweaty, sexy bodies molded together in the pale light of her bedroom, sprawled on the bed she used to sleep in when she came to visit her grandmother as a child.

A quick flip and she straddled him.

"Oh yeah. You remember how to ride, honey?"

She lifted her butt and let his cock slide part way out before she shifted again, sliding him back inside.

"Just like that. Hell yeah. Ride me, babe."

In no time, she set an even pace, bringing them both to the brink. Both of his hands stopped on her hips, as he helped her shift exactly how they both needed to bring them ever higher. She rested her palms on his chest, raking his nipples with her fingernails, enjoying the hiss escaping from his lips.

Heat rushed from her toes, up her legs, spearing through her abdomen. She climaxed on a cry, spilling desire over his cock.

"Yes, yes, yes," he panted, driving his erection into her several more times before finding his own release, her name on his lips.

She collapsed on his upper body until her breath semi returned to normal. His fingers brushed over her back, almost tickling her skin. He rolled them both over so she lay next to him, her head resting on his chest.

Moonlight filtered through the gauzy curtains on the window while his fingers traced a pattern on her arm, causing goose bumps on her flesh.

She didn't want to ask what happens now, but the words hung on the end of her tongue. The biggest question in her mind wasn't what happens between them but what about Kale?

"Spill it, darlin'."

"Huh?"

"I can hear the wheels turning in your mind from here," he said, kissing the top of her head. "I know you've stuff running around in your pretty head, so if you want to talk…let's talk."

"I don't want to talk right now, Cade. But, will you stay? Tonight, I mean. I don't feel like being alone. This house is huge, and I don't like the thought of being here by myself."

"Sure, honey. I'll cuddle up and sleep right here next to you."

"Perfect," she said in almost a purr.

Within moments, she drifted off to sleep with his big body curled around hers, and her hand slack on his abdomen.

Chapter Five

Grey skies met her eyes through the small opening in the curtains, when Natalie opened them the next morning. The warmth of the arm lying across her abdomen took her by surprise, for a moment, until she remembered Cade spent the night. Memories of their lovemaking rushed back, flushing her body with heat and embarrassment. She never behaved so wantonly with a man before. Begging for his touch, and crying out his name in her climax, just wasn't Natalie Bennington.

"You're thinking too much," he whispered against her ear.

"I didn't know you were awake."

"I kind of figured."

"Listen, Cade. What happened last night—"

"Was magnificent. I'd love to do it over and over with you."

"But I don't normally act like that."

"Good. I'm glad I made you lose control. Natalie, there's nothing wrong with what we did. We're both adults, and because we are, we can do what we want without permission from anyone."

She frowned and huffed out a small puff of air. His fingers grasped her chin, turning her head toward him. Soft blue eyes met hers, melting her irritation like snow on a hot summer day.

"You are a very sexy, beautiful woman."

A small snort left her lips, and she covered her mouth with her hand.

"You don't think so?"

"Put it this way. The last guy I was with, left me for someone younger, skinnier, and prettier."

"He's an idiot."

"You have to say that. We're lying here buck-ass naked together."

"No, I don't, Nat. Hasn't anyone ever told you how pretty you are?"

Her gaze dropped to his chin, but she refused to answer.

"Honey, look at me." When she raised her eyes back to his, he said, "I don't sleep with ugly women."

"Oh my God, Cade. You didn't just say that!"

"It's the truth. Your eyes are a gorgeous green and remind me of the sea. Your breasts fit perfectly in my hands." He palmed her breast and his thumb rasped over the nipple bringing it to an aching point. "You are the same age as me, and I don't feel old, so I guess it means you aren't either."

"Hazel. My eyes aren't green."

"They can be depending on your mood, darlin'."

A hearty laugh spilled from her lips. "Way to bring the heat down a notch, Cade."

The wicked grin on his lips brought a smile to her face.

"I could really use a shower. How about you?" he asked, waggling his eyebrows.

"Somehow I think there's more to this than the need to wash."

"Of course." Two fingers pinched her nipple, and she fought the moan bubbling in her throat. "Getting you naked—"

"I'm already naked, if you hadn't noticed."

"Mmm. Yeah, I kinda did. But I thought more like hot water tricklin' over your breasts, soaping your skin so it's slick to my touch, before bendin' you over and slidin' into your sweet heat from behind."

"Okay. All right. I get the picture. Sex in the shower."

"Not just sex. Sizzlin'..." He licked the seam of her lips. "Scorchin'..." He teased her ear. "Blisterin'..." He nibbled her neck. "Wicked shower sex."

Goose bumps dotted her flesh with every word he spoke. The rich, low growl of his voice with each syllable sent need zipping down her back to settle between her thighs. Her pussy throbbed with the racing of her heart.

"You know you want to," he murmured

She captured her bottom lip between her teeth.

"I promise I'll make you come at least twice."

"Twice?"

"Uh-huh."

Her fingertips tingled with the need to touch, to arouse him like he aroused her, and to make him feel this same unrelenting need to have him buried to the hilt inside her that she felt.

"First one in gets to adjust the temperature!"

In a flash, she jumped from the bed and headed for the bathroom with him on her heels. The sharp squeal coming from her lips surprised her when he scooped her up in his arms and stepped into the shower.

"Now what are you gonna do?"

"I like it hot. What about you?" she asked.

"Oh yeah. The hotter the better."

Steam rolled out of the open shower stall. Her grandfather built an impressive travertine tile shower with multiple showerheads pointing in several different directions. Natalie loved this shower, but sharing it with Cade brought on a whole new meaning.

"This is really cool," he said, checking out the different heads, adjusting each one to spray just right. "Did your grandfather put this in?"

"Yes and I love it."

Cade grabbed the pouf off the ledge along with the lavender scented shower gel. "So this is where the lavender scent comes from."

"Huh?"

"The sweet smell of lavender I've come to associate with you."

"Oh. Yeah. Probably so. I use it all the time and some of the lotion I use on my skin is lavender too."

The messy material foamed with the soap when he squished it several times. The soft slide of the bubbles over her skin, felt like heaven—across her neck and over her breasts. Inching his way from breast to navel and then through the curls at the juncture of her thighs.

"Mmm."

"Feel good?" he asked in a strangled whisper.

She couldn't help but notice his straining cock standing proud against his abdomen.

"You have no idea."

"Turn around and I'll do your back."

Warm spray beat against her chest as he ran the soapy implement over her back with one hand, kneading the muscles of her shoulders with his other.

"Wow. You are really tight."

"Lots of stress lately."

The bubbles disappeared with the spurt from the showerhead, but he continued to work the tight knots.

A soft moan slipped from her lips. His hands wandered down her back, continuing to roll his thumbs over the bumps and valleys of her body until he reach her ass. The next thing she felt was both hands on her breasts, molding the flesh to his palms and rolling the nipples with his fingers. Her head lolled back onto his shoulder. His cock pressed into the crack of her butt.

"Ever had a man in your ass, Nat?"

"No," came out in a moan.

"Want to?"

"Maybe. I've thought about it."

"Not right now, but it's something we'll have to explore."

"You're going to make me into a wanton woman, Cade Weston. No one will recognize me at all."

"And this is a bad thing?" he whispered. The rough pad of his tongue did delicious things to her neck while he continued teasing her nipples. His teeth nipped at her earlobe and one hand skimmed down her belly. "Open for me, darlin'."

Her thighs spread without thought, and she almost screamed as one callused finger slipped over her clit.

"Easy."

"No such thing," she panted. "God it feels good."

A whimper rose to her lips when both hands disappeared and he stepped back. She turned her head, blinking in confusion.

"Sit on the side there." His voice dropped an octave, and he almost sounded like he was having a hard time breathing.

She squeaked when her butt hit the cold tile.

"I'll warm you up in a second, darlin'. Put your butt right on the edge." She scooted closer. "Yeah, like that." He dropped to his knees, between her legs. "Oh my. So pretty. So pink." Her head fell back against the tile when he licked from slit to clit. A soft moan spilled out of her mouth. Two of his fingers found her pussy and slowly pushed inside. The high-pitched whimper didn't sound like anything she'd heard before. Well, maybe she had. Last night in fact.

His other hand pulled back the hood protecting the tight bundle of nerves. Her butt almost came up off the tile as he toggled her clit quick. The fingers inside her pussy pushed in and out. The whole scene felt surreal and like something out of a porn movie, but she didn't care. Cade brought her to the edge of climax, backed off on his ministrations long enough for her to settle down, and then brought her back up until she hung on by her fingernails. Frustrations made her ball her hands into fists, and then splay her fingers wide as she fought the rise and fall of her passion. She wanted to grip his hair and force him to bring her over the abyss. Desire coiled in her belly. Need zipped from her toes. Warmth spread up her legs, bursting through her pelvis on a scream as cum dripped from her pussy and over his fingers.

He kissed the inside of her thigh, nipped it with his teeth, and licked her clit one last time.

"One."

Heavy eyelids opened to find him grinning at her.

"Climax. I promised at least two."

"Uh, yeah."

She wrapped her hand around his cock and stroked up and down.

His breath hitched and she smiled. *At least he's not immune to my touch.*

"You're killin' me, darlin'. I want inside you so bad, I hurt."

"Then do it. Fill me up."

Her hand guided him to her pussy. Hot water sprayed over his head, running down his chest in rivulets. She took one of his nipples between her lips and sucked. The hard nub beaded against her tongue, and a hearty moan escaped his mouth. The head of his cock slipped a tiny bit inside, and he stopped with a quick inhalation.

"Condom."

His jaw clamped in frustration. The tick in his jaw told of his ability to hold his need in check without slamming into her without regard to protection.

"Are you clean?" she asked, her gaze boring into his.

"Yeah. I got tested a few months ago and I always use a condom."

"Me too. I'm on birth control."

"What are you saying, Nat?"

"Fuck me, Cade. I need you."

His eyes rolled back in his head. "But—" She planted her heels on his butt, pulling him close, pushing his cock deep inside her. "Ah hell," he growled as he grabbed both of her hips and began thrusting.

The feel of his cock sliding in and out of her pussy without the barrier between them, couldn't have felt more amazing. Hot, silky steel rammed home with each plunge. Every slide had her whimpering. Her pussy vibrated with his insistent lovemaking. Legs trembled. Pulses raced.

"Come for me, darlin'."

The rough gravel of his voice sent her over the edge, shattering her into a thousand pieces of sparkling light as she screamed his name.

Seconds later, his own completion reached its peak. His ragged breaths and rapid, jerky thrusts told her he couldn't hold back. She flexed the muscles of her vagina, and he groaned deep in his chest, climaxing on a rush.

"Oh God, Nat," he growled, burying his nose in her neck.

She trailed her fingers down his back while they caught their breath. The water started turning cold and she shivered.

"We need to get out of here before the water turns to ice. Your grandfather obviously didn't have a huge hot water tank."

"I'm sure he never expected his granddaughter to have sex in his shower either."

That got his attention. He groaned as he got to his feet and then pulled her up in front of him.

"You aren't sorry we did this, are you?"

"Sorry? No. Overwhelmed? A little."

"No need to be, honey." He kissed her nose and turned off the water. A big, fluffy towel hung from the rack on the wall within easy reach of his fingers. A moment later, he wrapped her in it and rubbed her down.

Once they were both dry, they went back into the bedroom and silently got dressed.

"Coffee?"

"That would be great," he replied.

"I'll make some while you finish dressing." The door opened with a twist of her hand, and she hurried down the stairs to the kitchen. Images and thoughts flew threw her mind while she filled the pot with water and added the grounds to the basket.

What the hell am I doing? I just had wild sex with Cade, both last night and this morning, but I have a date with Kale on Saturday. I should break the date. She chewed her bottom lip. *But I don't want to. Is it bad of me to want both of them? What would Cade say if he knew I still wanted to date Kale?*

"What are you thinking so hard about?"

"Sorry, I didn't hear you come in," she replied, her cheeks heating with embarrassment.

"Obviously. So are you going to tell me?" he asked. Both arms came around her waist and he pulled her to his chest.

Her gaze dropped to the center of his chest, and she fiddled with one of the buttons on his shirt.

One of his fingers slipped under her chin, forcing her gaze back to his.

"What if I said I still wanted to date Kale?"

* * * *

A fist to the gut would feel about the same. The sheen of tears on her lashes told him she wasn't sure about the whole thing and needed him to reassure her it would be okay.

"Honey, if you want to date Kale and me both, it's fine. We aren't exclusive." He raked his fingers through his hair when he stepped back. "Hell. We haven't done much dating ourselves except dinner last night."

"And sex."

"Yeah, and sex, but I don't want you to get the idea it means we won't see other people." For some reason he wasn't sure he liked that idea much.

"You and Kale seemed at odds last night at the hospital, and I don't want to come between your friendship."

"Let's play it by ear, okay? I know you have a date with Kale on Saturday. Go on your date and have a good time. If you want to have sex with him, go ahead."

Frown lines appeared between her eyebrows. "It wouldn't bother you if I had sex with him?"

I didn't say it wouldn't bother me.

A heavy sigh rushed from between his lips. "I'm not saying I would like it, Nat, but I need to tell you something about me and Kale."

The coffee pot sputtered and spit. "The coffee's done."

"Great. Let's grab a cup and sit down. I want to explain something to you."

She poured two mugs and brought them to the table along with sugar and cream.

"This is great, honey."

"So what is it you need to tell me?"

He took a deep breath and said, "You know Cynthia and Kale's wife left us to be together."

"Yes."

"Before the two of us married our respective wives, there was a time or two where we shared a woman. It's happened since our divorces too, once or twice."

"Shared? I don't think I understand."

"Have you ever heard of a ménage relationship?"

Her bottom lip disappeared between her teeth, and her eyes narrowed. Moments later, those same gorgeous green orbs widened in shock, and her mouth formed a small 'oh'.

"You had sex with her? Both of you? At the same time?"

He nodded and answered, "And there's been more than one."

"Wow," she whispered.

He could see the wheels turning behind those expressive eyes, but he stayed quiet, letting her think through it.

"How many?"

"How many women?"

"Yes."

"There's been ten total over the years. The last one happened a few years ago. It's not like we do it with every woman I date or he dates. The girl has to be open to the possibility, and we kind of try to gauge it if the occasion arises." He brought the coffee cup to his lips and sipped at the hot liquid.

"Have you thought about it with me?"

Coffee flew across the table as he spit the contents of his mouth.

"Gosh! I'm sorry, Cade. I didn't mean to make you choke or anything," she said, slapping him on the back.

"Its fine," he rasped in between coughs. His eyes watered, and he felt like a ten-pound weight was pushing against his chest. *Thought about it? Oh, hell yeah. Thought about it. Dreamed about it. Masturbated thinking about it.*

"Are you sure?"

He held up one hand, coughed twice, and motioned for her to sit back down. "We haven't discussed it in detail, Nat."

"What's that supposed to mean?"

"We've mentioned it to each other. Okay?"

"So you have thought about it between you—talked about it."

"Yeah, Natalie, we have. I really don't want to go into this right now, but —"

"Too bad, Cade Weston. You brought it up. I'm only trying to get answers. Now, I can either talk to Kale or you can be truthful with me."

"Fine."

"I want you to answer my questions truthfully and fully. Is that understood?"

Why he got the feeling this was her teacher persona, he wasn't sure, but all of the sudden, he felt like a high school kid again.

"I've never had sex with two men at the same time, obviously."

"All right."

"How does it work?"

He nervously cleared his throat before he said, "Most of the time, it starts with one guy and the second one joins in. There are a couple of ways it's considered a ménage. The term ménage can classify several types of relationships, but for me and Kale, it's always been the two of us and one woman."

"What's the other types?"

"Multiple women and one man or vice versa."

"Oh." Her lip disappeared between her teeth again. "All right. Go on."

"Normally, the woman has one...um...cock in her pussy and one in her mouth or in her ass." He stood abruptly and refilled his cup. This conversation made him horny as hell, even though they'd had sex not an hour before. He pressed his palm to his throbbing cock. *Down boy.*

"Sounds interesting."

Oh hell! She's actually contemplating this? I would never have thought she'd be game for two on one.

"Let's not jump into this, all right? I mean you and I had sex, yes, but you might not be interested in having sex with Kale."

She tipped her head to the side slightly and smiled. He didn't like that particular smile.

"Maybe. Maybe not. I won't know until I have some alone time with him."

Shit! I don't like where this is going.

The phone rang on the wall, and she got to her feet to answer it.

"Hello?"

Cade took his cup and moved back toward the table.

"Yes, Gram. We'll be on our way in a few minutes. We're having a cup of coffee."

The grimace on her face told him her grandmother figured out something.

"I know I said *we*, Grandma, but I'm not going to elaborate on the phone. We'll be there shortly." A short pause and she rolled her eyes. "Bye, Gram."

"Caught onto the *we* real fast, didn't she."

"Oh yeah. Nothing gets by her." Her cup made it into the sink. "Shall we go?"

"Sure." Several swallows later, he set his cup in the sink next to hers. They moved toward the living room where they dropped their coats the night before. "Can we swing by my apartment? I really need to change into something a little more casual."

Her gaze slid down his dress shirt and across the bulge tenting the front of his pants.

"Of course we can. Tight jeans on you are nice too."

"Wicked woman," he grumbled, but he couldn't help the smile lingering on his lips. *Saucy wench.*

The door closed behind them, and his hand settled on the small of her back as they walked to his truck. Inside the cab, silence surrounded them for the short ride to his apartment.

"Wow. You live here?" she asked as they pulled into the lot. His building actually consisted of an old store in downtown with some of the upstairs converted into apartments.

"Yeah."

"This is great. Where's your place?"

"Second floor. Come on. We'll go through the back. They have a great, old, cage-style elevator we use."

The back door of the building opened into a wide hallway. Bricks lined the walls and tile graced the floors. Wood accents, large potted plants, and gold gilded mirrors completed the picture.

"I thought you made it sound like this place was hardly anything to look at, Cade. It's beautiful in here. I can't wait to see your apartment."

"It's not much. A bachelor pad, if you will. I'm not here a lot."

"Kale said you stay at his place sometimes. Do you have your ménage sex there?"

Hell! This is going to get weird. I can't believe she keeps bringing it up.

"Um. Yeah. Sometimes there. Sometimes here."

He closed the cage on the elevator and up they went. The door to his apartment sat to the left of the landing. Wood paneling covered the walls on this floor, but the same tile lined the floors, and the same large plants and gilded mirrors graced the walls.

It didn't seem like much to him, but the wonderment in her eyes when he opened the door to his place, made him think twice.

"This is yours?"

"Yeah," he replied, trying to see it through her eyes.

His big leather couch took up one wall with a matching recliner on the opposite side of the living room. Heavy wood tables accented the couch and flanked the chair. A large brick fireplace engulfed one whole wall and glass hurricane lamps bordered the edges of the mantle. The state of the art kitchen, with its stainless steel appliances and granite countertops, appeared to the right from the entryway. The big bay window looked over the street below.

She walked to the window and pulled back the white curtain. "You can see everything going on in town from here."

"Yep. More than I want to sometimes."

"This place is fantastic, Cade. I'm glad you showed me," she said, coming back to his side and slipping her arms around his waist.

"Me, too." The brush of her lips against his brought his thoughts right back to getting between her thighs again. "Let me change real quick and we can be gone."

"Maybe I want to watch."

"You do that, darlin' and we'll be here another hour."

"Only an hour?"

"I've created a monster."

Her wild giggle followed him into the bedroom.

A short twenty minutes later, they stood at the door to her grandmothers' room at the hospital, and he had to smile at the sound coming from inside.

"I am *not* taking Xanax. I have no need for a sedative, and you will not force one on me, young man."

"But Mrs. Oliver, the doctor ordered—"

"I don't give a shit what that lame brained, bobble-head, piece of meat in a lab coat thinks. I have all of my mental faculties about me, and I will not bend to his will. Do you understand?"

"Yes ma'am."

Cade fought the grin on his lips, trying to cover it with his hand, but a matching one lingered on Natalie's mouth, too.

"You can tell him to find some other helpless old lady to stuff full of medication, but this one isn't doing it. Not today and not tomorrow!"

Natalie shook her head. "What are we going to do with her?"

"She's going to give them hell at the rehabilitation center."

"I know. Those poor nurses."

A roar of laughter left his mouth before he could stop it.

"Natalie Marie, is that you hanging out there?" her grandmother called.

"Yes, Gram," she replied.

"Well get your butt in here, girl. I want to find out exactly who *we* is."

Natalie glanced at him, tipping her head to indicate he should precede her.

"Oh, no. I'm not going in there alone."

"Chicken."

"Bauk. Bauk."

"Fine. I'll go first." She strolled inside, and he didn't mind the glimpse of her perfect little ass either. "Hi, Gram."

"It's about damned time you got here. What took you so long?" He walked in behind Natalie and her grandmother said, "Oh. I gotcha. How did the springs hold up on your old bed?"

"Grandma! Oh my God. You didn't just say that."

"Well you did, didn't you?"

Natalie's face turned bright pink.

"Never mind. You don't have to answer," she replied with a twinkle in her eyes. "How are you, Cade? How'd you sleep? Oh wait, good I would imagine if the red cheeks of my granddaughter tell me anything."

"Yes, ma'am. Quite well, thanks," he said, laying his hand on Natalie's shoulder. It bothered him when she shrugged out from under his grasp and moved toward her grandmother as if she wanted to get away from him.

"I would appreciate it if you didn't discuss my sex life, Grandma."

"If you didn't want me to know who *we* was, then you shouldn't have brought him with you."

"She's got you there, Nat."

"You aren't helping matters here, Cade," she told him and then turned back to her grandmother. "How are you feeling this morning? You seem irritated."

"I am *irritated.* The stupid, idiotic doctor thinks he can cram drugs down my throat and make me complacent so I won't fight him and his brainless decisions about my care. I want another doctor."

"Gram, no one will take care of you like grandpa did. You have to understand that."

"I know, Natalie, but I'm not going to let them drug me and shove me into some nursing home. I've decided I'm going home."

Natalie opened her mouth to protest, but Mrs. Oliver stopped her in her tracks.

"I've made my decision. I'm stronger today than I was yesterday, and I know my speech isn't quite as slurred. I can walk with a walker and get around some. We will bring in the physical therapist to the house. If you're staying, we can do it all there."

"All right, Gram. I'll take you home and we'll work it out."

Her grandmother patted her hand and said, "I knew you'd see it my way."

Cade shook his head, smiling when her grandmother winked at him.

"Will you stay one more day so they can evaluate your condition?" Natalie asked.

"Evaluate what? I'm fit as a fiddle."

"They'll need to have the physical therapist do some things with you to decide how best to proceed with your rehabilitation. Please stay one more day."

"All right. I guess I can't argue with you about it, but I won't take any drugs. I'm not letting them knock me out."

"Fine, Gram. No drugs to knock you out."

With a bit of a cocky smile, Mrs. Oliver settled against the pillows, asking, "So, was he good?"

Gratefully, he wasn't drinking anything, because, it would have been a repeat of earlier when he spit his coffee across the kitchen. Now, he knew where Natalie got her snarky remarks and her don't-take-no-shit attitude.

"I can't believe you just asked me how good he is in bed."

"Why not? He's a strapping young man. I think he could satisfy you pretty well. In the bed, in the shower, in the kitchen…"

"Enough, already," Natalie grumbled. "I'm not discussing my sex life with you."

Cade didn't think Natalie's face could get any redder. How could he have known the old lady would know where they'd had sex, or she did a damned good job speculating.

"Knock. Knock." All three of them turned towards the door, to see Kale poked his head inside. "Can I come in?"

Oh hell! How much did he hear?

Chapter Six

"Hi, Kale," Natalie said, shifting her gaze to Cade to gauge his reaction. She didn't like the stiffening of his spine. "Come on in. What are you doing here?"

Kale walked over and kissed her on the cheek.

"I figured I'd come by and see how your grandmother was doin' this mornin'. I didn't expect to see you here." He turned and stared at Cade. "Or you, Cade."

"Kale." The name sounded almost like a growl from Cade when he stepped in front of Kale. "I'm sure you noticed my truck in the lot. There aren't too many trucks with *Weston* on the tailgate."

"I didn't notice."

"Whatever," Cade grumbled.

"Enough you two," she said, stepping between them.

"Oh, let them go, Natalie. I love a good scrapin' between grown men over a woman." Her grandmother rubbed her hands together gleefully and then folded them over her chest. "I think you can take him, Cade."

"Grandma, will you stop encouraging them, please, for God' sake." Natalie put one hand on each of their chests. "You are not going to fight over me."

"We aren't fightin', Nat."

"You would if I let you, so knock it off."

Cade's cell jingled in his pocket. With a scowl and a grumble, he pulled it from his pocket, flipped it open, and growled, "Weston." His eyes narrowed and he turned towards the door to take his call.

"I'm sorry, Kale. I don't know why he's acting so possessive."

"Could be because you slept with him," her grandmother said. Natalie wanted the floor to swallow her whole, or a gag for her grandmother. She couldn't decide which at the moment.

"I see," Kale replied. "Well then."

"Can I talk to you a minute?"

He shrugged and said, "I guess."

"In private?" she asked, taking his hand and pulling him towards the door. "We'll be back in a minute."

"Take your time. I'll keep Cade occupied," her grandmother called as they walked into the hall.

They kept walking until they reached the end of the hall. When she turned to face Kale, her heart dropped into her stomach. Sadness stared back.

"Did you and Cade sleep together?" he asked, but uneasiness rang clear in his voice.

"Yes."

A long sigh escaped his lips and stuffed his hands into the front pockets of his jeans. "I guess there's nothing more to say then."

He started to walk away, but stopped in his tracks when she said, "He said he didn't care if we went out or even if we had sex."

Kale turned back around and gave her a wide-eyed look. "He did?"

"Yes." She took his hand in hers. "What happened between me and Cade just happened. It wasn't planned. But it doesn't mean there is anything permanent, lasting, exclusive, or whatever you want to call it, between us."

"Wow."

"You know what else he told me?"

"No."

"He told me you two share on occasion."

She almost laughed at the choked look on Kale's face. His eyes bugged and he coughed several times. "He did?"

"Yeah. But he also said it had been awhile." She glanced to her left and then to her right. Several doors on patients' room stood open. "I'm not discussing this here, in the middle of the hospital, but you and I need to talk. I know we have a date on Saturday, but I want to talk to you before then. Can we have dinner tonight?"

"Uh, sure. I'm free."

"Good. Now let's go back to the room and see what other kind of chaos my grandmother is starting with Cade."

They walked back into the room in time to hear her grandmother telling Cade the end of the story about how her grandparents met and married. "My daddy hated ole Doc with a passion, and he swore if he ever showed his face at my daddy's place again, he would fill his ass full of buck-shot. It didn't stop Doc though. He walked right up to the house, told my daddy he was takin' me to the next county, and we were gettin' married."

"Sounds like Doc," Cade replied. He turned around, noticing they returned to the room. "Nat, I'm sorry, but I have to go. My foreman called and one of my horses is havin' some trouble. I need to check it out."

"It's fine, Cade. I'm sure Kale will take me home."

His lips firmed into a straight line, and she could tell he didn't like the thought of her alone with Kale at all. *Mmm. Interesting.*

"Of course I will," Kale added. "I'd be happy to."

"See? Everything will be fine."

"I hate to leave you like this, darlin'." The look in his eyes said it bothered him. *So much for not caring if I date Kale.*

"I know you have to go, Cade. I understand. You have business to tend to and you've already spent a lot of time with me." She reached behind his head and brushed her lips over his. The pressure of his mouth felt marvelous, and she hated to stop the kiss, but the audience present made it impossible to do anything more. "Call me tomorrow or something."

"All right." With one last look at Kale, Cade left the room with the soft click of the door closing behind him.

She cleared her throat and turned back toward her grandmother. The mischievous twinkle in her eyes made Natalie nervous. If it's one thing she came to realize since she'd been back in Red Rock, her grandmother wasn't your typical old lady.

"Grandma, butt out," she warned.

"I don't know what you mean, Natalie. I'm not doing anything."

"Well, listen. I need to get going. I have some things to do at my place before our dinner date tonight. Do you want me to take you home?"

"No. It's fine, Kale. I want to visit my grandmother for a bit before I head back to the house."

"I promised Cade I would take you home."

"I'm a big girl. I can call a cab. You go on."

"What time do you want me to pick you up?"

"Five?"

"Sounds perfect." After a quick kiss good-bye, he disappeared too.

"You're having dinner with Kale?"

"Yes, Grandma."

"But you had sex with Cade."

"Yes, I did. But Cade and I aren't exclusive. I've only been back in Red Rock a few days, and I haven't been out of my relationship with Steven very long either."

"Then why did you have sex with him?"

The heavy sigh rushing from her lips sounded hollow, even to her own ears. "Everything would be too difficult and lengthy for me to explain, Gram."

Her grandmother hoisted the head of the bed, settling back against the pillows. "I'm not goin' anywhere. Spill it."

Natalie knew she wouldn't get out of telling her grandmother the entire tale of what happened between her and Cade, but she wasn't about to give her explicit details.

"I'm attracted to Cade. Hell, I'm attracted to Kale too."

"I believe that is rather obvious."

"This whole thing is rather funny, you know? Neither of those two gave me the time of day in high school."

"Go on."

"When Cade helped me out with my car on my way into town, I thought it was only for old time sake. Then he asked me to have dinner with him. I don't know whether Kale asked me for lunch yesterday because Cade asked me on a date first or what. I feel like I'm being torn in two by them. And I don't want to ruin their friendship. I'm afraid this is turning into some kind of competition. Who can get the shy band girl to fall in love with them first?"

"In love?" her grandmother asked with a raised eyebrow.

"I'm not in love with either of them, so don't get your hopes up. I can't seem to get either of them out of my head. Last night just happened. Cade took me to where he's building his house. It's beautiful up there, Gram. He has it set back in the trees with a huge pasture in front. The framework and stuff is already done. He said he was building it for his family."

"Nice."

"Listening to him talk about how his wife would be able to look out the window of the kitchen and watch their children playing in the yard or how they could look out the front and see the cows and horses grazing in the pasture—it made me want to be that woman."

"It sounds like you have feelings for Cade already."

"I don't know, Gram. He's gorgeous, sweet, and smart. Everything a woman could ask for."

"All right then, what about Kale?"

"They are such opposites in looks, and Kale is all those things too."

"But?"

"Nothing. I'm confused. Cade told me he didn't care if I dated Kale or even had sex with him."

Her grandmother frowned and said, "I wouldn't be surprised if he didn't mean it at all."

"I know what you mean." She stood and walked to the window. Cars sped past below her, and she wondered if anyone slowed down to feel the passion in the wind, the rain on their face, or the love of their family these days. If someone asked her a year ago if she'd be standing here in Red Rock, trying to decide over two different men, she would have told them they'd lost their mind. "I read somewhere once that men can have one-night stands or casual sex and it doesn't mean a thing to them, but women are emotional creatures. It's difficult for us to be in a relationship under those circumstances."

"You know I'm here for you, honey, no matter what you decide, whether it be one, both, or neither."

The both part snapped Natalie's head around, staring open mouthed at her grandmother.

"I'm not sure you are aware of this or not, Natalie, but your mother dated two men at the same time."

"She did?"

"Yes. It shocked the entire town. It went on for a while. Almost a year, I think, before she finally settled on your father."

"Great. Now I'll be stirring up old rumors and whispers, when people around here realize the connection of me and my mother."

"You never were one to follow convention, sweetie. Don't start now. If it requires you dating both men to decide which one is better suited to you, then so be it, and to hell with the busybodies in town. They'll find something else to gossip about in no time."

She walked back to the side of the bed and hugged her grandmother. "Thanks, Gram. I love you."

"I love you, too. Now, get you a cab and head back to the house. You've got a date with one handsome man in a few hours."

"I'll be here in the morning to pick you up and take you home. Please, don't give the nurses a hard time."

"Me?" Her grandmother batted her eyes innocently.

"Don't give me your innocent look. I know better." Natalie kissed her on the cheek. "I'll call you later."

"Sure, honey. Have fun tonight."

* * * *

For the next several hours, Natalie paced like a caged animal. She tried on every piece of clothing she owned, but nothing seemed right. Without knowing exactly where they were going for dinner, she had no idea what to wear. Kale seemed more of the laid-back kind versus Cade. The nervous anticipation skipping through her body did nothing to help the situation. She finally decided earlier in the afternoon to forgo going out somewhere and found a couple of steaks in her grandmother's freezer. Food always seemed plentiful in the house. Fresh vegetables, fresh fruit, makings for salad, a couple of potatoes for baking, and dinner would be grand.

Five o'clock arrived with a dong of the doorbell, and she jumped in response.

Her palms felt itchy and damp. The hair on her neck stood and chills rolled down her back.

"This is nuts."

The door opened with a sharp tug of her hand.

"Hi," Kale said. "Can I come in?"

"Please." A quick flick of the lock on the screen and he stood close enough to smell. *Oh Lordy. I love the scent of his cologne. Something spicy and all male.* "Um. I couldn't find anything to wear so I decided to cook for you, if you don't mind."

"Mind? Honey, I haven't had a home cooked meal in ages. No way do I mind a beautiful woman putterin' around the kitchen makin' me food."

"Great. Come on in. You can drop your coat on the sofa. Would you like a beer?"

"Your grandmother keeps beer?"

"No silly. I ran to the corner store and grabbed some," she said with a laugh. "Of course, she could very well be a beer drinker sometimes. Hell, I don't have a clue."

"You didn't get to spend a lot of time with her growing up after you moved, huh?"

"No, and I'm sorry for it now. The last couple of days with her have been fabulous. When I go back to Portland, I'll have to make sure I come for visits often."

"But you'll be staying a while now, right? I mean, with her needing help around here and all."

"I'll be here for a few more weeks anyway. It all depends on how well she does with her rehabilitation. We won't know until she's done it for a week or so."

She grabbed two beers from the refrigerator, popped them open, and handed him one. Their fingers brushed, and her fingertips tingled from the contact. Not quite the same reaction she had to Cade, but interesting, all the same. After a sip of her beer, she motioned for him to follow her back to the living room.

They took seats, side-by-side, on the couch. "I've already got dinner in the oven. I would have grilled, but it's a bit cold out there," she said, running her sweaty palms down the thighs of her jeans.

"Don't go to any trouble on my account," he replied, with a squeeze to her knee.

"No trouble at all. How about a movie? Gram has a pretty decent DVD collection."

"Sure."

"Why don't you pick something and I'll check on dinner. I'll be right back." Her quick escape to the kitchen gave her a moment to think and breathe.

How in the hell am I going to bring up this threesome thing with Kale? I know he mentioned something yesterday during lunch, but since I had the conversation with Cade, everything seems kind of strange.

"You okay in there?"

"Yes. I'll be right out. I'm sticking the potatoes in the microwave." *Breathe, Natalie, breathe.*

After taking care of her tasks in the kitchen, she moved through the doorway to the living room, stopping in her tracks. Kale had turned the lights down low, and with the sun setting so early in the winter, it made quite a romantic picture. A fire burned bright in the fireplace, crackling and popping to the music he put on the stereo. Garth Brooks crooned The Dance softly in the background.

"I decided I didn't want to watch a movie with you right at this moment. But I'd love to dance with you."

"Here?" she asked in a small laugh.

"Of course. At least here, I don't have to worry about other cowboys cutting in because you're the prettiest girl in the place."

"You can compliment me all you want. I don't mind."

Laughter echoed in the room, and he pulled her tight against his chest. "I love it! You're great."

He took her right hand in his left, allowing his other hand to skim down to her lower back. The soft music continued to play and she lost herself in the feel of being in his arms.

"This is nice."

"Mmm. I think so too," he murmured, brushing his lips against her ear.

"Kale," she whispered.

"Hmm."

"We need to talk."

"Yeah, I know."

"Cade and I talked—"

The ping of the microwave interrupted her trail of thoughts.

"I think that's the potatoes," he said.

"It is," she replied, stepping out of his embrace. "The steaks should be about done too. Would you set the table?"

"Sure."

The warmth of his hand at the small of her back, sent tingles down her legs. When they reached the cupboards, she grabbed place settings for two and handed him everything he needed to set the table. A low whistle came from his lips to the tune on the stereo as he set the plates and silverware out.

She pulled the meat from the oven, the potatoes from the microwave, and the vegetables from the stovetop. "Why don't you grab the plates and we'll fix them over here."

Plates in hand, they moved back toward the table together. He set his down and held her chair.

"Thanks."

"You're welcome."

"You know, it's funny. Men in Oregon don't do those kinds of things."

"Things?"

"Hold doors, pull out a lady's chair…you know gentlemanly things."

"See. You should move back to Red Rock so you can be treated like the lady you are." His smile devastated her control. Dimples peeked out of his cheeks, she hadn't really noticed before. The five o'clock shadow coating his jaw line tempted her to touch, to feel the scrape of his whiskers against her fingertips, and to lose herself in his lips on her hand.

"If it were only that easy."

"You can live where ever you want, Nat."

"At the rate I'm going, I'll be here a while. I'm not sure how my grandmother is going to do here in the house." She folded the napkin in her lap. "Luckily, they already turned one of the downstairs rooms into a bedroom when grandpa was sick."

"Have you talked to your mom about all of this?" he asked. His tempting lips wrapped around the beer bottle when he took a long draw.

"No and I probably won't. She's going to be majorly pissed at me about it, but my grandmother doesn't want me to call her, and I feel it's her choice, not mine."

"Your grandma is a hoot."

A hearty chuckle left her lips. "You aren't telling me anything I haven't figured out. I never know what will come out of her mouth next."

Watching his face, she wasn't sure what to make of the looks passing over it. At the point of her mentioning talking to Cade, he appeared annoyed.

"I really didn't want to bring this up during dinner, but I need to get this off my chest."

His gaze dropped to her breasts, and she cleared her throat to bring his attention back to her face. "I didn't mean those."

"Sorry," he said with a sheepish grin. "Can't help it. They are rather nice."

"The girls' thank you, but we need to talk seriously here."

"All right." The fork full of potato disappeared between his lips, waylaying her thoughts for a moment.

"Cade and I talked about the two of you sharing."

"Sharing what?"

"Don't act like you have no idea what I'm talking about, Kale. Sharing a woman."

The frown on his face did nothing to alleviate her uneasiness.

"What exactly did Cade tell you?"

"You've done it ten times—sometimes at your house and sometimes at his apartment—a few of times before you both married, and a couple times since the divorces. But it's always with the acknowledgment and consent of the woman involved."

A heavy sigh left his lips in a rush and she smiled. He apparently didn't like this conversation much.

"Sounds like he explained things pretty well."

She nodded. "Yes, he did. I want to hear your side of things and if you two talked about having said type of relationship with me."

"You?"

"Yes, me, Kale. Don't look so surprised. I'm not a complete idiot. I know men talk, and if you two have done it before, then I want to know if you discussed doing it with me."

The look on his face was almost funny, as his cheeks flushed with color.

"You're embarrassed."

"A little." He jumped to his feet, pacing the kitchen floor. "I'm not the type of man to talk to a woman about bedding her." His fingers cut a path through his hair. "You told me earlier, you and Cade already had sex."

"Yes, we did. Last night and this morning."

"Twice?"

She looked away for a second then focused back on his face. "Well, yes. He spent the night last night and it happened."

"Shit."

"It doesn't matter, Kale. The issue I'm having right now is my attraction to both of you. Handsome doesn't come close to describing you two. Either of you can have your choice of women, I'm sure, and I am beyond thrilled to think you are attracted to me."

"Why wouldn't we be, Nat? You are beautiful, sexy, smart, and sweet. You're the type of woman every man wants to come home to after a hard day's work."

"Thank you. But you are avoiding my questions."

His fingers trailed through his hair again, leaving several strands sticking up, and she wondered why she felt the need to smooth them back into place.

"All right, yes. Cade and I discussed it right after he found you out on the road. The next morning, in fact. Neither of us really went into detail."

"How do you feel about sharing?"

"If the woman is accepting to it, then I'm good with it. It can be an amazing experience for her, but also for the guys involved."

"Cade described to me how it works."

"Thank God," he murmured, and she couldn't help but smile. *Poor guy.* He seemed so uncomfortable talking about this; it almost made her want to let it go. *Almost.*

"How would you feel about me having sex with both of you?"

"Do you want to have sex with me?"

"I don't really know, Kale. We haven't had much time together, you know, getting close, cuddling and all."

"Have you had time to do those kinds of things with Cade?"

"Things just happened with Cade. He showed me his house, and he's been a rock for me with my grandmother. We came back here after all the turmoil from yesterday and things heated up from there. Now, I want to spend time with you and find out if this attraction I feel can lead to something more."

"I'd like that too."

"Good. Come finish your dinner. I didn't mean to cause an issue while we were eating. I'm comfortable with you, Kale, and if nothing else, I think we could have a really good friendship."

He grimaced and shuttered.

"What?" she asked.

"The *friendship* word."

The laughter bubbling from her lips sounded more like the Natalie she knew. Serious conversations like this weren't part of her personality, but she felt it needed saying. "I didn't mean it. I swear!" She held up both hands in surrender as giggles still filled the room. He grabbed both of her hands in his and kissed her quickly.

"Good. Let's finish this fabulous meal then we can watch a movie, go out for drinks, dance, or whatever. Anything you want to do, but it has to afford me the opportunity to wrap my arms around you and get close. I want the same chance you gave Cade."

Kale kept the conversation light, making her laugh the rest of the meal. Serious didn't fit the description of his personality at all. She did remember him being more of the class clown when she lived here during her childhood. Joking around and never taking things too seriously was his specialty.

"You remember Mrs. Baxter, right?"

"The English teacher?"

"Yeah. You probably didn't know it, but she started dating the football coach."

"Mr. Alexander? You're kidding me, right? Those two couldn't be more opposite. She was, um, what's the word I want? Frumpy, I guess, and he was the handsome jock. He had all the female students panting after him, even if most of us in school were jail-bait for him."

"Guess what? They're married now."

"You're kidding? Really? Wow!"

He nodded. "I believe they had a baby a couple years back, too."

"I would never have pictured those two together."

"Me either, but I guess it goes back to opposites attract sometimes."

"What about you? Do you want kids someday?"

"Yeah, I'd like to have a couple anyway. My ex never wanted kids. I didn't realize it until after we'd already been married a year and I mentioned it to her. You would have thought I'd asked her to carry an alien inside her or something. She freaked."

"To each his own, I guess."

"Do you want kids, Nat?"

"Of course. I'd love to have several, but I need a husband first. I don't believe in having a child until there is a loving relationship to bring them in to. I've seen way too many one-parent households with my students. It's a major struggle for the children and the parents." She grabbed their plates and took them to the sink. "Let me quickly wash these and we can take our drinks into the living room."

"Let me help."

"Really?"

"Sure. My mother did raise me to help around the house. I even cook sometimes."

Both hands planted on her hips she tapped her toe. "I thought you said you hadn't had a home cooked meal in ages."

"Oops. Busted." He shrugged and laughed. "I meant, by a beautiful woman. I do cook for myself, but it's not the same." His lips brushed her nose and he pulled her close. "Mad at me?"

"No."

"Good. Can I kiss you now?"

"Do you want to?"

"More than anything on Earth right now."

The warmth of his breath on her face had her toes curling in her shoes. The wicked little smile on his mouth made her heart skip a beat. When he brought his lips closer, hers started to tingle in anticipation. He'd kissed her before, but not an all consuming, passionate, melt-your-panties kind of kiss and that is what she wanted.

One hand slid into her hair. The other held the side of her face. He nibbled at the sides of her lips, sweeping his tongue over the seam of her mouth, before plunging inside when she moaned. Both of her hands went around his neck, and she tilted her head to fit their mouths together better. Tongues explored the insides of each other's mouths, licking, entwining, and stroking. Each diving and retreating.

His hands slipped down her back, tugging her close enough her breasts brushed his chest as her nipples tightened. He tasted good—damn good.

When he finally sighed and pulled away, she wanted to chase him down and bring him back.

"Some kiss," he murmured, pressing his forehead against hers.

"Yeah."

With a rough clearing of his throat, he took her hand and pulled her toward the couch. "Do you want to stay here, or do you want to go out somewhere? The honky-tonk down the street has a live band tonight."

The phone on the end table jingled, and she frowned. "I wonder who that is." Her grandmother didn't own anything close to being high-tech, so no caller ID. "Hello?"

"Hey, Nat."

She glanced at Kale and replied, "Hi, Cade."

Chapter Seven

"Is everything okay over there?" Cade asked and she had to shake her head.

"Of course. Why wouldn't it be?"

"I wanted to check in with you. Is Kale there?"

"Yes, Cade, he is. We're sitting here on the couch."

"Doin' what?"

"None of your business, mister."

"Well, I—"

"Give me the phone a sec," Kale said, taking the receiver from her hand. "Cade? I didn't butt in with your time with Natalie, so quit butting into mine."

She smiled, shaking her head and glancing down at her hands where they lay in her lap.

"She's in perfectly good hands with me, and put it this way, I won't do anything you didn't do. Nighty-night." He shut off the phone, stood up, and unplugged it from the wall. "The hospital has your cell phone number right?"

"Yes."

"Good. Cade doesn't, does he?"

The laughter in her chest just about burst free. "No."

"Perfect."

"You." She chuckled. "Unplugged." The giggle turned into a full-blown laugh. "The phone."

One of his eyebrows shot up and she couldn't help it. Her stomach hurt from laughing and she doubled over.

"I didn't think it was that funny."

"I'm sorry, Kale," she gasped. "It's not. But the jealousy on your face is."

"Jealous? I'm not jealous. I've never been jealous of Cade."

When her giggles finally calmed, she said, "How do you feel knowing I had sex with Cade before you?"

"Before? Are you saying you plan to have sex with me?"

"Answer my question."

"All right, yeah. It bugs me some, but I'm willing to forget about it. But you have to be willing to give me the same chances."

"I'm here with you tonight aren't I?"

"Yeah."

"Then you have the same chances he had. You can woo me, love me, and sweep me off my feet, too. I have to warn you though. You have your work cut out for you."

"Why?"

"Sit down and I'll tell you about some of my past relationships."

"Okay."

Once he took his place next to her on the couch, she said, "I dated my ex for a couple of years. His name is Steven. He's the father of one of my students—well, he used to be. I haven't had his daughter in my class in two years."

"Awkward."

"At first, yes. He asked me to dinner, and I tried to explain to him I didn't date my students' parents."

"Persistent, wasn't he?"

"Very much so. I finally agreed to have dinner with him. One thing led to another, and we ended up sleeping together the first night, which I don't normally do."

"But you slept with Cade last night on your first date."

"Thanks for reminding me."

"Sorry."

"Anyway, he became my whole world. I loved his daughter as if she was my own. We moved in together, and I thought everything in my life had come together. I loved my job. I loved him, and I thought he loved me, until I went to a conference in Seattle. The conference ended earlier than expected, so I came home a day before he expected me. I wanted to surprise him, but I got the surprise of my life when I walked in on him with another woman, in our bed."

"Wow."

"Yeah."

"What did he say?"

"He didn't make excuses. He said he had wanted out of the relationship for a while. I wasn't what he wanted in a wife."

"What the hell did he want?"

"Someone younger, skinner, and prettier. The woman in our bed was a new partner in his law firm. She recently joined them straight out of law school."

"He's an idiot."

A dry chuckle left her mouth. "Cade said the same thing."

"We agree on one thing then." He kissed her nose. "I think you are a very special woman, Natalie, and I'm thrilled to be here with you tonight. If something happens between us, then so be it. I'm not pushing. Would I like to make love to you? You're damned straight, but it'll happen when and where we choose and not before."

"I appreciate you giving me time."

A frown crossed his face. "Are you going to sleep with Cade again?"

"He doesn't know it yet, but no. I need to figure out what is between you and me, and me and him, before I sleep with him again. It's not fair to put that kind of pressure on a budding relationship."

"I'm glad to hear you say those words." He wrapped one arm around her shoulders and pulled her to his side. "I don't want to have to kill my best friend."

"Oh, stop it, will you," she said, punching him in the side.

"Ouch."

"Pleeaassee. I did not hurt you."

"My pride," he pouted then laughed. "Shall we watch a movie or go to the bar?"

"How about we go to the bar for a little while then come back here and watch a movie. It's still early."

"Sounds good to me." He brought her to her feet with him, shooing her to get her purse and a coat.

Snow fell in big flakes, coating their hair and jackets. The bar was only three blocks from her grandmother's house, and since it wasn't too frigid outside, they decided to walk. Hand-in-hand, they strolled down the sidewalk, taking in the sights. Christmas lights adorned almost every house. Big, inflated Santa Claus', twinkling lights of every color, nativity scenes in every size and shape, and some decorations so elaborate, they took your breath away, graced yard after yard. Christmas happened to be her favorite holiday. She frowned as she wondered if grandma would even decorate this year with grandpa gone.

"What do you want for Christmas?" Kale asked, bringing her thoughts back to him.

"Oh, I don't know. I love the holidays. It's my favorite time of year. I love to decorate, bake, and have a big family dinner on Christmas Day. You know all those family type things."

He tugged her close to his side. "Sounds like a great Christmas to me. I hope you'll still be here."

"I probably will with everything going on, and I really don't have anything to go back to Oregon for, except my parents and sister."

"All the more reason to stay here."

Within fifteen minutes, they stood outside the big double doors of the Saddle Club as loud music waved and ebbed every time the doors opened.

"Shall we?" Kale asked, holding one for her.

The band's attempt at God Bless The Broken Road by Rascal Flatts wasn't too bad, but it wasn't like the original either.

"They aren't terrible, huh?" hollering over the music as he nodded toward the stage.

"Not terrible, no, but the original band is much better."

The soft chuckle next to her ear sent shivers down her back. "I'm sure they are, but those big bands, like Rascal Flatts, don't come to Red Rock."

"Maybe someday they will."

"Let's dance," he said, pulling her toward the dance floor.

Several sets of eyes followed their path, making the hair on her arms stand on end. Kale put both hands on her hips and pulled her in close. She laid one on his chest while the other went around his neck.

"Damn, I love the way you smell," he murmured, his lips pressing to the soft skin beneath her ear.

"Lavender."

"Mmm."

"Cade and I—" His head came up so fast, he about knocked her unconscious, and she immediately apologized. "I'm sorry, Kale. I didn't mean to bring him up while with you."

Two fingers pressed against her lips. "Shh. Don't worry about it. You spent most of today with him. It's understandable to relate things that happened today with his presence."

She kissed his fingers then pulled them away from her mouth. "It's not fair to you. I promise, I won't bring him up again tonight. All right?"

The beat changed into a two-step with a fast rhythm, keeping them scooting across the floor. Kale twirled her and brought her back into his arms as he set their steps into motion. The bass guitar and the beat of the drums, thumped to the beat of her heart. Sweat tickled along her scalp. It had been some time since she danced like this, and the exertion had her breathing a little hard, or was it the man holding her?

"You're a pretty good dancer."

"Even two-steppin'? I haven't done this in ages."

"They don't two-step in Oregon?"

"Not much. You can find a few country bars, but not too many, and I'm not usually the bar-hopper type. I do like a beer now and again though, and the atmosphere of the honky-tonk is kinda cool sometimes."

"My kind of girl."

She bit the inside of her lip as his words seeped in. The uneasiness she felt in continuing to encourage this thing with Kale, made her feel like a heel. *Decisions. Decisions.* Choosing between the two of them got harder and harder with each passing day and every moment spent with them. Maybe it would be better if she went back to Oregon. If her grandmother had a live in caregiver, she wouldn't need to stay. Her ordinary, lonely life back home awaited her, but somehow, the thought wasn't comforting at all.

"You're thinking too hard," he whispered in her ear.

"Sorry."

"What's the frown for?"

"Can we sit? Or maybe it would be better if we went back to my grandmother's house."

"If you'd rather, its fine with me," he replied as they stopped dancing.

"Yeah. I think so. I think some alone time would be good."

"I'm all for alone time." A small chuckle left his mouth before he leaned down, brushing his lips against hers. "Let's go."

A few moments later, they stepped outside to see the snow coming down in a heavy blanket of white.

"Wow. It's really snowing now."

"How about I call a cab to take us back to the house?"

"No, let's walk. It's not very far," she replied, taking his hand and pulling him into the snow. "Besides, it makes it better to warm up when we get back. A nice fire, a little hot chocolate or coffee, soft music, and some snuggle time."

"Sounds like the perfect way to warm up after a walk in the snow. Besides, by then, my hands will be like icicles, and I'll need somewhere to warm them up. Along your hot body comes to mind."

"Hot, huh?"

"Oh hell yeah," he said with a wicked grin. He tucked her hand in the crook of his elbow as a saucy whistle left his lips. She couldn't help the smile on her mouth. His easygoing personality and take no shit attitude seemed to be just what she needed right now.

Once they reached the house, she unlocked the door and flipped the light on. "How about you build the fire back up and I'll get the coffee started. I think there's even some apple pie in the refrigerator."

"Apple pie? With ice cream?"

She shook her head, smiling at his little boy enthusiasm. "Yes, with ice cream."

"You gotta a deal, babe."

With the coffee finished and the pie dished up, she balanced the plates in one hand and the mugs in the other as she pushed the swinging door between the kitchen and living room with her butt. The crackle and pop of the fire seemed cheerful and bright. Kale had returned to the couch, but when she came through the door, he jumped to his feet to help her.

"Let me get those," he said, grabbing the coffee mugs.

"Great fire."

"It helps having good kindling and dry wood."

"I can imagine. I don't know the last time I had a real fire. My parents' place has a gas fireplace."

"Gas is for sissies."

Her laugh sounded dry and brittle. "Yeah. It's not the same as a log fire."

"With the snow falling outside, a warm cup of coffee, and some awesome apple pie? I'm in heaven here."

She kicked off her shoes and tucked her feet underneath her. "How's the pie taste?" The groan and satisfied smile on his mouth gave her the answer. "I guess that means good?"

"I haven't had pie this good since I went home last."

"How long ago was that?" she asked, slipping a bite into her mouth.

"Two days ago."

She laughed so hard, the plate jiggled in her fingers. "You are so busted. I'm so going to call your mother." The frown lines settling between his eyebrows and the fake frown on his lips made her laugh harder. "Typical man. Afraid of his mother."

"You're damned right. My father knows who tows the line in their home and it's not him," he replied with a deep chuckle. The sound sent shivers down her arms. She loved his laugh.

"So tell me. What kind of woman are you looking for?"

"Well, let's see. My ex came from money, and she expected us to live as her parents did. She didn't quite get that it takes time to establish one's self and have money coming in regularly. I had the jobs, but they weren't steady.

I supplemented our income with breaking horses. She hated the lifestyle, hated living so far out of town. I didn't want to hobnob with the social circles in Red Rock and she did."

"I find myself more of a homebody, too. I like going to movies sometimes, at the theatre, or going out for coffee because I can, but it's not a normal thing. I don't go out a lot," she replied.

"I would love to find a woman who is comfortable with herself enough not to worry about going to the store without makeup on, someone happy in jeans and a t-shirt, who likes riding horses, dancing, and enjoys going to barbeques. A woman that doesn't mind if I hang out with the guys sometimes and can find happiness in the little things—the laughter of a child, the snow falling, the wind in the trees, the sparkle of the sun on the lake, or the freedom of the wild horses running across the open plains."

"You are a hopeless romantic, Kale."

His cheeks flushed pink, and he dropped his gaze to the pie in his hands.

"You're blushing."

"I can't help it. I don't take compliments well. Never have."

The warmth of his skin under her palm felt good. The crisp, dark hair on his forearm, tickled her hand. "Well let me tell you. You're one special guy."

"Special enough you could fall in love with?"

* * * *

What the hell am I doin'? Scaring the hell out of her, that's what! Disgusted with himself over his behavior, he slid his plate onto the coffee table and grasped her hand in his.

"I'm sorry, Natalie. I shouldn't have said something so personal or pressure you in such a way. It's not fair to you."

Her hair felt like silk between his fingers when he tucked a stray curl behind her ear.

"No, it's not, Kale. I'm having a hard enough time dating both of you, but I forgive you. You are kind of at a disadvantage since Cade and I already had sex."

"Thanks for bringing that up."

"Crap. I'm sorry now. I shouldn't have brought it up again."

"I know he's already made love to you, and I want to more than anything in the world, but I think we need to take some time to get to know each other better. Rushing isn't my style. Of course, I don't have six months to woo you either."

"Six months?"

"Yeah. I don't sleep with a lady unless I've known her for a few months." The softness of her skin under his fingers made him want to stroke every inch of her, from the top of her head to the toes on her feet. Desire raced down his back, settling in his balls.

"Really?"

"I'm not much into one-night stands, Nat. It's not the way I am. Some guys can sleep with a woman without any kind of emotional ties—not me. I need to feel something for her before I sleep with her."

"I've heard men can have sex without emotion where women tend to need the emotional closeness."

"I'm fine with kissing you and holding you right now. Don't mistake it for not wanting you beneath me." Their eyes met and held. The green of her gaze appeared intense, hot, and full of emotion. "I want nothing more than to feel your heat wrapped around me, but I'll wait for the right time."

And for some reason, I don't want to discuss a threesome including Cade right at this moment. The thought irritates the hell out of me.

"How about a movie? I picked one out earlier and popped it into the DVD player, but since we ended up doing something different, I left it alone."

"Sounds like a great idea to me. What did you pick?" she asked, snuggling into his arms and throwing one leg over his.

"Die Hard."

She sat up with a start, her eyes wide with shock. "My grandmother had Die Hard?"

The look on her face made him laugh. "Yes, she did. Every last one of them too. We could have a Die Hard marathon tonight."

"There's what? Four of them, right?"

"Yep."

"At approximately two hours each, so that makes eight hours of movies with no pee breaks, no food breaks—um, I think I'll pass."

"All right. How about two of them tonight. It's six thirty now and four hours of movies would make it ten thirty."

"Sounds good, but I'm going to need sustenance. I'll have to check the kitchen for snacks."

"We had dinner about an hour ago, besides the pie and ice cream, so I should be good for a bit. How about we watch the first one and then worry about snacks."

"Works for me," she replied, snuggling into his arms again as he switched on the television and DVD player.

The roar of the opening credits filled the room with sound drowning out anything and everything but the hum. Action flicks were his favorite, like any guy he knew. Chick flicks tied women in knots, but he did give into those occasionally, depending on the woman. For Nat, he would watch a chick flick.

A soft lavender smell reached his nose, and he inhaled her scent, holding it inside, and savoring it for a while.

Stray strands of her hair tickled the underside of his chin. The pillow softness of her breast molded to his chest where she lay against his side. Her hand rested on his stomach and he fought the groan rumbling inside. If she moved her hand just a little, she would brush against the achy fullness behind the fly of his jeans. The need to have her cup his cock and stroke it about drove him insane. Her warm thigh pressed against his. His fingers slipped from her shoulder, down her arm, and back. The silkiness of her skin made him ache to taste and take pleasure in everything about her.

"You okay?" she murmured.

The warmth of her breath skipped over his skin. He wanted her lips. Everywhere. He cleared his throat and squeaked, "Uh. Yeah."

"You don't sound okay," she replied, tipping her head back.

"I'm fine. The smell of your hair is driving me crazy. That's all." Her tongue peeked out and slipped over the surface of her lips. "You're killing me here."

The smile creeping across her mouth looked almost wicked. *Did women do wicked smiles?* He didn't know, but decided hers qualified.

Her hand pressed to his chest, and she scooted back so they were nose to nose. "I want your mouth."

"Where?"

"Here," she whispered, tapping one finger to her lips. "Knock my socks off."

The growl coming from his mouth didn't sound like anything he'd heard before, but it definitely sounded possessive, and he didn't care. Kissing her could be his downfall—throwing in the towel—giving up the goose, or all of the above. He couldn't help himself. Tasting her became a priority as he lowered his mouth to hers.

The soft groan came from one of them, but he couldn't tell who. It seemed to float between them, passing back and forth from her mouth to his. Her tongue tentatively touched his lips and he opened for her with a moan. Women didn't usually come on to him, and he found it refreshing for Natalie to pursue him to some degree. He knew she needed to see the differences between him and Cade—feel what it was like to kiss him, make love with him. Finding out if the attraction burning between them could hold a candle to what she shared with his best friend became imperative.

The kiss deepened with a small tilt of her head. His fingers threaded into the tendrils of her hair and held her in place. Her lips were soft and felt perfect under his. She shifted so she lay across his lap, but never broke the kiss. Chest to breast. His cock stiff and aching as it pressed into her hip. He wanted to cup her breast in his palm and rake his thumb across her nipple, but he refused to give into his desire and hers. Pushing her would be a mistake. Giving into her would be a death-null.

He lifted his head and stared into the pools of green. "Nat, honey, we need to stop this."

"Why?"

His forehead met hers as he fought the urge to throw caution into the wind. "I don't want you to make love with me only because you are comparing me and Cade."

"But I'm—"

The brush of his lips stopped her words.

"You had sex with Cade last night and this morning. I want us to get to know each other better before it happens between us. Can you understand?"

She didn't look happy, but she nodded and scooted back.

Great going! Now she'll feel like shit for coming onto me.

"Please, don't feel bad, Natalie. It has nothing to do with my attraction to you. If I thought it would be you and me, without Cade between us, I'd throw you over my shoulder and haul your ass upstairs right now." He grasped her hand, pressing it to his aching erection. "Can you feel how badly I want you?"

"Either that or you've got one hell of a big rock in your pocket."

Loud laughter took the tension down a notch or two. "I know where you get your sense of humor, but God woman. I can see I have to watch everything I say for fear you'll turn it around and bite me on the ass with it."

Her eyes sparkled and danced with mirth. "Bite your ass? Uh-huh. Sounds like fun."

"I'm not saying another word." The zipping motion across his lips made her laugh.

"Let's enjoy the movie, and we'll leave the heavy petting and necking for another date."

He nodded, but didn't reply as he continued pressing his lips tight together.

One eyebrow shot up in a saucy I-don't-think-so look right before she twisted and straddle his hips. She was right where he wanted her, even if he refused to tell her so. Her teeth nipped at his lips, and he fought the smile trying to break free. Her tongue snaked out, licking the seam, but he refused to open. Changing her direction of attack, she slid her lips over his cheek until she reached his ear. Teeth nipped at his earlobe then sucked it between her lips. Still, he refused to utter a sound. He never realized how sensitive the skin below his ear was until she bit it softly before continuing her trek down his neck. The collar of his shirt gave way to the insistent push of her nose.

When the hell did she work the buttons loose on my shirt?

Before he knew it, the material parted, and her fingers began working his left nipple. She pinched and pulled on the responsive nub while biting and licking his neck and shoulder. The hot, insistent throb in his balls drove a whimper from in his chest to his throat, but he refused to release it.

"Talk?"

He shook his head.

"Oh, you are so screwed, buddy."

If only she meant what she said.

She pushed the material off his shoulders, continuing her journey down his chest until her lips closed over his right nipple.

His eyes rolled back and his head lolled against the back of the couch.

Damn, she likes to bite!

Her teeth scraped the hardened bud and desire clenched at his balls. His fingertips itched to pull her head tighter against him, but he refused to give into the yearning. His hands curled into fists. He wouldn't give into the feelings she stirred unless she made the first move. This sure felt like the first move to him.

The jingle of her cell phone interrupted her play.

"Shit."

"What?"

"Nothing I did made you talk, but my cell phone ringing did? Wow."

The phone rang again.

"Ignore it."

"I can't. It's my mother."

Chapter Eight

The phone continued ringing while she hunted for her purse. "Damn it! Where the hell did I put it?"

"On the end table," Kale replied while buttoning his shirt.

She fumbled with the latch, scrambling to grab it before it went to voicemail. "Hi, Mom."

"What took you so long to answer the phone?"

"I...um...I'm busy."

"Where's your grandmother? And why isn't anyone answering the home phone?"

Shit! Kale unplugged it.

"How do I say this without you yelling at me?"

"What's wrong? What happened? Spill it, Natalie Marie."

"Calm down, Mom. Grandma is fine, but she's in the hospital."

"Hospital? What the hell is going on over there?"

"It appears she had a small stroke."

"I'll be there tomorrow," her mother said, almost shouting into the phone.

"No, Mom. Grandma doesn't want you here. That's the reason I didn't call you. She wouldn't let me. She's doing fine. The hospital is releasing her tomorrow to come home."

"Home. How can she go home, Natalie, if she had a stroke?"

"It's not serious. She's a little weak on one side, but I'm staying, and we are going to have a physical therapist come in and work with her here at the house." She rolled her eyes as she glanced at Kale. With clothing back in place, he almost looked perturbed. His irritated steps took him back and forth in front of the fireplace while he raked his fingers through his hair.

"Well, tell your grandmother I don't care if she doesn't want me there. I'll be on the first plane in the morning. You'll need to pick me up at the airport. I'll call you when I know what time."

Great! This is just what I need, my mother hovering.

"Mom, really. You don't need to come. Everything is fine here. I'm taking care of grandma."

"Exactly what happened? Did she fall or anything, complain of weakness?"

Natalie bit her lip and tried to think of something to say that wouldn't give her away.

"What aren't you tell me, Natalie?"

"I wasn't exactly here when it happened, Mom."

"You weren't there? What in the hell are you doing? You went there with specific instructions to help your grandmother finalize everything and bring her back here to live with us. God, can you do anything right?"

"Thanks, Mother. I really appreciate the support. I'm sorry I let you down. Do whatever you want because obviously I can't measure up to your standards." With a soft whimper and a tear streaking down her cheek, she snapped the phone shut with an irritated click.

"Come here, honey," Kale said, wrapping his arms around her and pulling her to his chest.

She buried her face against his shoulder and cried like a baby. Her mother rarely got to her these days, but sometimes, she couldn't help thinking how much of a bitch she could be.

"Shh. It's fine. Whatever she said to upset you can't be bad enough to cry over." His strong hands moved over her back, soothing her and bringing her tears to a stop.

"It doesn't matter, Kale. I'll never be good enough for her."

The callused pad of his thumb wiped away the remaining tears from her cheek. "Why do you think that?"

Two steps back and her legs hit the couch before she sat down, crossing her arms over her chest. "It's always been clear. I wasn't the boy she wanted. For Andrea, it didn't matter. She was the second born. The first born had to be a son, which obviously, I'm not."

The couch sunk when he took the seat next to her, pulling her into his embrace. "You are definitely good enough. Don't let her negative attitude bring you down. You're a beautiful, intelligent, sexy woman and any man would be thrilled to call you his own. Your mother will come around eventually."

"I doubt it, but thank you for saying such nice things."

"If I didn't believe they were true, I wouldn't say them." One finger under her chin brought her face around so their eyes met. The chocolate brown of his, sparkled in the firelight.

"I think you should go, Kale. I'm sorry. I'm not real good company right now," she whispered, afraid he would try kissing her again. Her hands rubbed up and down her arms.

"If you want me to, Nat, I'll go."

With a stiff nod of her head, she gave him her answer. It would be better if she were alone tonight after the dressing down her mother gave her. If her mother would indeed be flying into Red Rock tomorrow, she needed her strength to deal with her, and right now, her heart wasn't into figuring out her feelings for Kale or Cade.

"Can I see you again?" he asked as he stood.

"Of course."

"How about Saturday still, since this one was an unexpected date?"

"All right. Dinner and a movie?"

"Sure. I'll pick you up about six?"

"Sounds perfect. See you then."

"Do you have some way of getting to the hospital to pick up your grandmother?"

"Yes. Her car is here and I have the keys. I'm all set."

"Good. Call me tomorrow once you two are back here, safe and sound. I want to know you're okay. These roads can be tricky."

"Even though I haven't lived here in a while, Kale, I have driven in snow."

"Oh yeah, when?"

"I used to ski Mount Hood every winter."

"With plowed and sanded roads leading right up to the ski area, I presume."

"Well, yes."

"Not the same as driving around here and you know it. Just be careful, babe. I don't want you in the hospital, too."

"I will, but I'll call you when we get back here."

"Good. Walk me out?"

"Sure," she replied, taking his hand in hers.

The snow had stopped, except for an occasional flake here and there, but a good quarter of an inch covered the ground. Her boots crunched in the snow with each step. No Christmas lights decorated her grandmother's home this year, and she made a mental note to ask about putting some up. Lights always made the season seem more real to her.

Kale wrapped both arms around her, tugging her close. "Can I kiss you good-night?"

"I'd like it if you did. Things kind of got interrupted in there."

"Yes they did, but I'm glad they did. You definitely had my attention and things were moving pretty fast."

Heat crawled up her neck and splashed across her cheeks.

"No need for embarrassment, Natalie. I was enjoying myself with the attention, but we already discussed waiting to make love."

"I know, but you threw the challenge out there, and I'm not the type of girl to back down from a challenge."

"I gathered that," he replied, chuckling softly.

Seconds later, she parted her lips to accept his kiss. Man, did the guy know how to kiss. Is it a prerequisite to being a hunk? Knowing how to kiss a girl out of her panties?

His tongue snaked inside her mouth, stroking along her tongue and fueling the fire. A soft moan left her lips as she tipped her head to take more. After several moments of light-your-underwear-on-fire kissing, he lifted his head, kissed her nose, and stepped back.

"I'll talk to you tomorrow."

"Uh, yeah. Tomorrow."

"Sleep well," he said, blowing her a final kiss.

When his truck backed out of the driveway and disappeared down the street, she sighed, shaking her head. Time. Time to think and analyze these feelings would be a great idea.

"A hot bath, lots of bubbles, and a hot romance novel. Mmm. Sounds like a perfect way to unwind from all of this and relax."

Back inside the house, she plugged the phone back into the wall, turned off her cell phone, and headed up the stairs. The bathroom she and Cade made love in that morning also held a huge tub, big enough for at least two people. Lavender bubble bath, hot water, a big fluffy towel, clean pajamas, and she had it made.

A soft sigh escaped her lips as she sank into the hot water. Long, hot soaks were not a pleasure she often affords herself, but what the hell. She didn't have anywhere to be right now. No man to worry about, no papers to grade, and no television shows to miss, so an extended warm bath could be the ticket necessary to focus.

Grandma is going to be so pissed if Mom shows up tomorrow, but I have a gut feeling she will. She never knows when to butt out and leave people alone. The groans spilling from her mouth sounded almost animalistic. Muscles relaxed. Her arms felt heavy and her eyes closed.

"I think she's more than open to the idea, Kale." Cade's voice boomed off the walls in the bathroom.

"Maybe. We didn't get a chance to discuss it earlier," Kale answered.

"Well I did and she seemed totally fascinated by it." Cade's lips brushed hers. "Natalie, honey, do you want us?"

She moaned, shifting in the water.

"I take it that's a yes," Kale replied.

Two naked bodies slipped into the bath with her, splashing water over the sides of the tub. Cade's hand palmed her right breast and Kale's took her left.

"So round. So perfect," Cade whispered in her ear. "We're gonna make love to you, Natalie. Both at the same time. I want your perfect round ass and Kale wants inside your hot little pussy."

Her nipples pulled tight under their fingers. Cade raked his thumb over the sensitive tip, and Kale rolled the other between his finger and thumb. Her back arched and she whimpered in need.

Cade's fingers abandoned her breast and skimmed down her belly to slide between her legs. "Open for me, darlin'."

Thighs parted. Whimpers rose and fell from her mouth uncontrollably as the two men brought her higher and higher. Kale's lips closed over her nipple. His teeth and tongue did delicious things, sending desire zinging from the tip to her clit. Cade pushed two fingers into her pussy. "Oh yeah. Hot and slick."

Desire spiked hard. "Oh God!"

"Tell us what you want, Nat," Kale murmured in between tonguing her nipple.

"I want both of you inside me. Please."

Kale leaned against the tub, grabbed her hips, and pulled her so she straddled him. One swift plunge sheathed him deep inside her, causing her to throw her head back and groan. "Yes."

"My turn, darlin'," Cade said, moving between Kale's slightly bent legs.

"Cade," she moaned.

"What, honey?"

"Now, please." His cock bumped against her tight back hole.

"Easy. You said you've never had a man there before."

"I don't care. I want you inside me."

Kale shifted his hips, sliding in and out several times, fucking her hard.

"Easy Kale. Let me in man."

"Hurry up. I'm about to blow here."

Cade pulled her ass cheeks apart and slid two fingers inside. She whimpered and pushed against his hand. "You like that?"

"God, yes. More. I need more." His fingers disappeared and the head of his cock brushed at her entrance. "Please, Cade."

A sharp, loud ringing brought her upright in the tub.

"Holy shit! I was dreaming?"

The phone rang again and she almost cried. There would be no satisfying the sexual frustration running through her body without the help of a man or maybe two.

"Hello?" she groaned into the phone, hoping it wasn't her mother again or her grandmother.

"Nat, darlin'. Are you okay?" Cade asked on the other end.

"Cade," she breathed. "Thank God you weren't my mother."

"You sound out of breath. Did I interrupt something? Is Kale still there?"

"The only thing you interrupted was my bath, and no, he isn't here. He went home about an hour ago."

"I almost came over there. You weren't answering the phone, and I don't have your cell number."

"Everything is fine, Cade. You don't need to come over here."

"What if I said I wanted to?"

Maybe I should. I mean, I know he could take care of this problem I have now, but I told Kale I wouldn't until he had a chance with me too.

"I would like nothing more than for you to come over here, Cade—"

"Great! I'll be right there."

"But no."

"No?" The surprise in his voice almost made her laugh.

"No. You shouldn't come over here. There's nothing you can do for me right now. I'm going to get out of the tub..." He groaned deep into the phone. "And get ready for bed. Alone."

"Ever had phone sex?"

"Excuse me?"

"Phone sex, Nat. You know. We talk. You make yourself come and I do the same. Are you game?"

"Seriously?"

"Yeah. Why not? Even if we did have sex earlier today, you just talking makes me hotter than hell."

"I am horny," she murmured, drying off.

"Why? Kale?"

"Actually, yes and no. I've been over that for a while, but I had one really great dream while I was in the bathtub."

"A dream, huh."

"Yep."

"Care to tell me about it?"

"Let's just say you and Kale were both in it."

"Oh?"

"Uh, yeah. And remember how you told me about how you two work a threesome?"

He replied in a choked, "Yes."

"Put it this way, I have a really vivid imagination."

"Aw, fuck."

"Mmm. Yeah, you could put it like that."

"Are you sure you don't want me to come over?"

"I'm sure, but I think the phone sex thing could take care of my problem and maybe yours."

"What are you wearin'?"

"Nothing."

The low growl through the phone made her smile. "You?"

"Right now? Jeans and boxers, but give me a second." The shuffle, zip, and whoosh of his clothes were loud on her end of the phone. "Okay. Now, nothin'."

"I need to go into my room. Hang on a sec." She unplugged the bathtub, wrapped the towel around her, and moved toward her room. "Do I need my vibrator?"

"Depends."

"On?"

"Do you think I can make you come with my voice?"

"I think I'll skip the vibrator and make you work for it, stud."

"Oh, honey, you asked for it." He cleared his throat, dropping his voice an octave. "Are you stretched out on your bed?"

"Uh-huh."

"Take your right hand and move it over your right breast."

A soft moan left her lips when she did as instructed.

"Roll your nipple between your fingers like I want to do. Can you feel it? Feel my fingers."

"Yeah," she breathed.

"Wet your other fingers with your tongue then swirl it around your other nipple. That's my tongue, darlin', swirlin', and lickin' at the pretty little pink nub."

"God, Cade. You're pretty good at this."

His chuckle on the phone brought her down a notch.

"My hand is sliding down your belly to part those full, pink lips."

Her breath hitched.

"Swirl your finger around your clit."

"Mmm," she hummed.

"Perfect, darlin'."

"Are you coming along with me, Cade?"

"Oh, you know it. My cock is so hard, I could pound nails with it right now."

"Stroke it for me. Feel my warm hand wrapped around you, sliding up and down."

"Toggle your clit for me, honey." Cream slid between her ass cheeks. "Are you wet, Nat?"

"Definitely." She captured a little of the silky wetness, using it to lubricate her ministrations on her clit. "It feels like your tongue."

"My, my. Naughty girl."

Rasping breaths in the phone matched hers. She knew he bordered right there with her. Her motions quickened. Pressure increased. Her legs tingled with the pressure to come.

"I'm gonna come, Cade. Come with me."

"I'm right there, darlin'. Fuck, this is so hot."

Pleasure rushed up her legs and burst through her pelvis on a flash of need so strong, she cried out and heard his answering moans in her ear. Several moments of rasping breathing told her he needed a minute to return to normal, too.

"Was it good for you?" she asked with a giggle.

The warm chuckle told her the whole scenario didn't bother him at all and she needed that—needed to know he was okay with out of the ordinary, because, her life, at the moment, seemed anything but ordinary.

"So do you want to tell me about your dream?"

"Not unless you plan on getting me off again over the phone."

"I don't think so. I'm wiped and I need a shower. It's been quite a while since I've had phone sex."

"Feeling old, Mr. Weston?" she asked

"Hell no. You make me feel like I could do anything, darlin', includin' keepin' you well satisfied in the bedroom."

"I hate to say good-bye," she whispered, feeling the loss of him already.

"I know, but you should probably get some sleep. I'm sure you need to be at the hospital bright and early in the mornin'. If you aren't, your grandmother will flag down some trucker and hitch a ride home."

"Yes, she would, but I've got other things on my mind too. My mother will probably be flying in tomorrow."

"Your mother? Why?"

"She called earlier and I couldn't help but tell her about Gram. She came all unglued and said she would be on the first plane out of Portland and would be here some time tomorrow."

"Your grandmother isn't gonna like that at all."

"You aren't telling me something I don't know, but my mother won't listen to me. I tried to tell her."

"It'll be okay. The two of them will have to hash it out between them, and I wouldn't bet on your mother winning."

She laughed and rubbed her nose. "No. I'd bet on my grandmother any day of the week."

"You're a lot like her, you know."

"My grandmother?"

"Yes. You've got her spirit and spunkiness."

"I appreciate the sentiment."

"You're welcome. Now, I'm goin' to head to the shower. You get some sleep."

"Yes, sir."

"I kind of like it when you talk all submissive."

"Don't get use to it." The laughter in the phone had her shaking her head. "Good-night, Cade."

"Night, darlin'."

* * * *

The sun rose bright and early the next morning. Blue skies peeked through the thin layer of clouds, and for now, it appeared there wouldn't be any new snow today.

Natalie got up early, showered, dressed, and grabbed two cups of strong coffee before heading to the hospital to pick up her grandmother. The old Buick sitting in the garage had to be something out of the nineteen-eighties, but she knew her grandmother loved the old car. Thankfully, the town plowed the roads after last night's snow.

"Good morning, Gram," she said, breezing through the door with a smile on her face.

"What's so good about it?"

"I see you're in a wonderful humor this morning," she replied, kissing her grandmother on the cheek. "No handsome male nurse to give you a bath?"

"*Hrmph.*"

"You're speechless? That's a first."

Her grandmother stuck out her tongue and Natalie laughed. "Don't get your panties in a wad, granddaughter. Speechless, I'll never be."

"I believe you, Gram. So what's the issue already?"

"Your mother."

"Oh shit."

"Yeah, oh shit. She called bright and early to inform me she would be flying in today to take care of me. I don't need her here and I don't want her here."

"I know, Gram. I'm sorry. I didn't have much choice but to tell her what happened. She called the house last night and wanted to talk to you."

Her grandmother patted her hand. "No worries, honey, I'll take care of her. I may be old, but I sure in the hell ain't dead yet, and she's not about to take over my life. I know she left you with specific instructions on what to do while here. I don't have any plans to allow anyone to bully me into leaving my home."

"Mom doesn't stand a chance, does she?"

"Hell no. I raised her and I know what to do with her. If she doesn't like it, she can get her ass back on a plane and go right back to Oregon."

She couldn't help but smile. Her grandmother had more spunk and grit than a lot of people she knew. "Has the doctor been in yet to discharge you?"

"If he had, do you think I'd still be sitting here in this flimsy thing they call clothing?"

"No, Grandma, I imagine you wouldn't be. You would already be dressed and sitting downstairs, tapping your foot."

"You're damned right I would."

"What did the physical therapist say?"

"Read it yourself," she replied, waving toward the packet of information on her tray table.

Natalie picked up the paperwork and scanned it. Three times a week with the in-home physical therapist and exercises to do on her own. The percentage of weakness on her right side didn't seem too bad, but she wasn't a medical professional.

"Are you prepared to do these exercises everyday like they suggest?"

"If it means your mother not coming, of course."

"You know you can't avoid it. She's coming whether you want her to or not."

"And we'll go rounds when she gets here. You can count on that, because I don't want her here."

"Hopefully, she won't stay long."

"How about if she turns around and goes back on the same damned plane she comes here on?"

"Somehow, I don't think she will, Gram."

"What do you think she'll say when she finds out your dating two men? Oh, by the way, how did the date go with Kale last night? Anymore hot sex?"

"I'm not discussing it with you," she replied, taking the chair across from the bed.

"Oh, come on, Nat. Let an old lady live vicariously through you."

"You'll survive, Gram and no, I did *not* have sex with Kale last night." *I'm not about to tell her I had phone sex with Cade.*

"Well, damn it girl! You had the perfect opportunity."

"Can you imagine what my mother would say finding out I'm dating two men, much less, if I had sex with both of them?"

"It's none of her business, Natalie. You're a grown woman, and you can make your own decisions on who you want to see and who you want to sleep with."

"I know, but she's so controlling. She loved Steven. She had a huge fit when she found out I broke it off with him. It didn't matter to her I caught him in bed with someone else."

"And we both know my opinion of him."

She laughed and shook her head. "Yes, Gram, we do."

Both eyebrows shot up almost to her hairline. "Your mother expected you to stay with dick-wad even after he screwed another woman in your bed?"

"Yes. She told me it must have been a mistake and men have those kinds of weaknesses. I needed to forgive him and seek counseling."

"Counseling, my ass! The man cheated on you. There is no excuse for that kind of behavior in a relationship. Never once did your grandfather ever look at another woman, much less, have sex with someone else in our bed."

"The relationship you had with grandpa is the kind of loving connection I want with my husband. I'm not going to settle for less. I refuse to be complacent in a marriage."

"Good for you, honey. The right man is out there for you. He may not be Cade or Kale, but you'll find him, if you don't settle. Never settle for anything except the real thing."

She captured her bottom lip between her teeth.

"Spill it, Natalie. You're holding out on me," her grandmother said, crossing her arms over her chest.

"Don't tell Mom I told you, but my dad cheated."

"Your dad had an affair with another woman?"

"Yes. Several years ago, I believe, but she smoothed it over, forgave him and everything."

"And?"

"He still cheats on her, but she chooses to ignore it now."

"Wait until she gets here. I'm going to kick her ass for her!"

"Well, good morning ladies. How are we this morning?" Doctor Bridges said as he came through the door. "Ready to go home, Mrs. Oliver?"

"Damn right and it's about time you got your ass off the golf course and got me out of here." Her grandmother flipped the covers off her legs and threw them both over the side of the bed. "Get me my walkin' papers and we'll be on our way."

"You know it will take a few minutes, Gram, so calm down."

"She's right, Mrs. Oliver. I've written the orders for your discharge, but it will take a bit for the nurses to get the paperwork ready. Sit back and relax for a bit."

"They can get up off their lazy butts and get it done. I know they are all sittin' around the nurses' station gossiping about who you are sleeping with this week, Doctor Bridges."

The man coughed and looked at her, but she only shrugged.

"I'll...um...see what I can do to hurry them along," he replied, walking backwards toward the door.

"You do that and I'll get dressed. Get my clothes out of the closet there, Natalie. I want out of this place."

"I know you do, Gram. Hang on and let me help you."

"I'm not an invalid."

"Yes, ma'am, I know."

She prayed they would hurry with the paperwork. Her grandmother wouldn't be patient long. By the time she dressed and tied her shoes, the nurse came through the door with her discharge papers.

"You don't need to go through all of it, miss, I know what it says."

"Mrs. Oliver. I am required by law to go over this paperwork with you and make sure you understand the instructions. I have to sign my name to it saying you understand. Would you like me to put my license on the line?"

"No. I guess not, but hurry up."

In no time, they had her bundled up and inside the old Buick.

"Be careful, Natalie. I don't want you to wreck my car."

"I will, Gram."

"Go slower."

"Grandma, I know how to drive."

"I realize you do, but this is my car, and no one has driven my car since your grandpa got sick."

With a shake of her head, they drove out of the parking lot and started down the main street. If she kept the conversation going, maybe her grandmother wouldn't harp on her about her driving. In no time, they were pulling into the driveway at the house.

"I wonder whose car is sitting on the street. I don't recognize it," her grandmother said as Natalie turned off the ignition.

"I'm not sure."

Seconds later, they found out when Natalie's mother came barreling out the drivers' side door, yelling at the top of her lungs. "Natalie Marie! You're supposed to be here taking care of your grandmother, not dating half the eligible bachelors in Red Rock and sleeping with the other half."

Chapter Nine

"Oh hell," Natalie groaned. "I thought she wasn't coming until later?"

"Obviously not," her grandmother replied.

"Hello to you too, Mother."

"Don't hello me, young lady. I've got words for you."

"Butt the hell out, Marie. She's done nothing wrong. The only thing she's done while she's been here is take care of me and have a little fun."

"A little fun? A lot more fun than she needs to be having. She should be on the phone with Steven, trying to work things out, not dating whoever takes her fancy," Marie said, standing with her hands on her hips and tapping her toe.

"Steven is an asshole. And we aren't discussing this in the driveway." Her grandmother took her arm and said, "Help me inside, honey."

"Get her things from the backseat, Mother."

"Wha—"

"You heard her, Marie. Get my things from the backseat while she helps me into the house."

"Well, I never."

"I imagine that's part of your problem," her grandmother replied and Natalie chuckled softly. "If you had some good sex once in a while, you wouldn't be so uptight."

The chuckled turned into a full-blown laugh at her mother's expense.

Once in the house, she helped her grandmother sit on the couch and moved toward the kitchen to make coffee, giving her something to do with her hands, other than strangle her mother, but she could still hear the banter in the other room.

"You need to mind your own business, Mother."

"To hell you say. Natalie is having a good time while she's here, and I see not a damned thing wrong with it."

"She wasn't sent here to have a good time."

"No, she was sent here to wrap me in a straight-jacket if necessary and cart my ass back to Oregon."

A minute or two of silence followed her grandmother's words, and Natalie could imagine her mother's mouth opening and closing like a guppy. The whole scenario made her giggle. God, it felt good to laugh. It had been a while since she'd felt like laughing.

"I'm not going back to Oregon, Marie. I'm completely competent, so trying to say I'm not, won't work. I know every attorney and judge in this town, and there isn't a one who will say I can't take care of myself. You might as well get your ass back on the plane and go back to your low-life of a husband."

"Low-life? What are you talking about, Mother?"

"Natalie told me about Gerald cheating on you. If you are stupid enough to stay with him when he's screwing around with whatever bimbo catches his fancy this week, then you aren't the woman I raised you to be."

Shit! She wasn't supposed to say anything.

"You are a beautiful woman, and you shouldn't be treated like you have no brain-cells in your head. You're intelligent, caring, and have a wonderful heart for those less fortunate than you. Quit letting him take advantage of you, Marie. He dragged you away from your family. Had you hold up in the god-forsaken suburb of Portland. Pushed you into living a life you didn't want and forcing your children to live a life away from God's country. This is where you belong, not in Oregon."

Silence met her ears as she strained to hear anything her mother said to her grandmother's accusations.

"Mom, I'm sorry. You're right."

"Halleluiah and praise the Lord."

Natalie grabbed three cups of coffee, and the cream and sugar. Her eyes welled with her grandmother's speech, and it broke her heart to know her mother suffered for her and Andrea. Never had her mother said a word about being miserable, but since her grandmother pointed out the facts, she could see it plain as the nose on her face.

"Anyone want coffee?"

Marie silently wiped her eyes, and nodded while her grandmother took one of the mugs from Natalie's hands.

The jingle of the telephone on the end table brought her head around to stare at it and wonder who might be calling now.

"Aren't you going to answer it?" Marie asked as she set her cup down on the coffee table.

"Uh, yeah." Natalie grabbed the phone and said, "Hello?"

"Hey, darlin'."

"Hi, Cade."

One of her grandmother's perfectly painted on eyebrows shot up in a wide arch and a huge smile spread across her face. "Invite that hunk on over here."

Natalie shook her head no and narrowed her eyes on her grandmother.

"I take it your grandmother is home safe and sound."

"Um…yeah and my mother is here."

"Oh great. I bet it's a nice family reunion," he replied.

"Uh, no," she told him into the phone. "Gram, I'm going to take this in the other room."

"Oh?" her mother asked, her fingernails tapping on the edge of the ceramic mug. "Why not talk in here, Natalie?"

"I'm not talking to Cade in front of you, Mother. This is a personal call." She spun on her heels and moved toward the kitchen. When she picked up the receiver she said, "You can hang up, Gram."

"Damn it. I thought I was quiet enough you wouldn't hear me," her grandmother replied with a laugh. The hanging up of the receiver clicked in her ear.

"So your mom is there, huh?"

"Yes, unfortunately. She's already started in."

"About?"

"Evidently, my mother got wind of my dating while I've been here."

"Oh. Not good."

"Yeah. I've already received the raised voice and 'how could you' talk, and she hasn't been here an hour yet."

"I called because I wanted to see if you would like to go sledding day after tomorrow. Since your grandmother is home now and your mother is there to help, you could sneak away for a couple of hours."

"I don't know, Cade. It's probably not a good idea. I don't need to give my mother anything else to lecture me about."

"The snow should be perfect—all fluffy from the snowfall last night and it's supposed to snow again tomorrow, but be clear the next day. Great sledding weather. The sun should be out and it's not supposed to be frigid cold. I would love to keep you warm though."

"All right, I tell you what. Pick me up at ten. We need to talk anyway."

"Talk? That's not exactly what I had in mind."

"I know it's not, but we need to anyway."

"Great. See you then," she replied.

He softly said goodbye and she hung up the phone.

"So Cade's coming over, huh?" her grandmother asked from the living room.

A heavy sigh escaped her lips, and she dropped her head back. "Eavesdropper!" she yelled with a laugh.

"What can I say? You talk loud."

"Not that loud, old lady!"

"Natalie Marie!" her mother exclaimed.

"Oh give it up, Mom. Grandma and I are two of a kind."

Her grandmother let out a roaring laugh, and Natalie had to smile. It was good to hear.

"Sledding?" her grandmother asked. "Sounds like fun."

"I haven't been sledding in ages. I go skiing sometimes, but never sledding."

"It'll be good for you then. Cade's a nice man."

"Yes, he is, Gram." She took a seat next to her grandmother and asked, "What shall we have for dinner tonight?"

"A nice, big, juicy steak sounds wonderful."

"I'm sure the doctor recommended dietary changes with your stroke."

"I'm not changing my diet to suit his idea of what the hell I should eat."

"Grandma, be serious please. You know you'll have to cut back on the red meat and work on your cholesterol levels. He gave you several prescriptions to help with those things, but you need to make changes too. Exercise and eating right are important to your recovery." Natalie bent closer to her ear. "And you don't want Mom sticking around any longer than necessary, do you?"

"Oh, hell no!" her grandmother exclaimed. "She can go back to Oregon any time, and don't let the door hit you in the ass on the way out, Marie."

"Mother, I know you don't want me here. You've made that perfectly clear, but—"

"But you don't give a shit what I want or whether I need you here or not. Natalie and I were doing just fine without you."

"Natalie wasn't even here when you had your stroke. She was out with some *cowboy* from Red Rock who only wants to get in her underwear," Marie snapped.

Natalie watched grandmother's eyes narrow and her face pull into an angry glare.

"My granddaughter's behavior is none of your business. I told her to go out and have a good time. You are the idiot who is trying to get her to go back to dick-wad. Leave her alone and let her do what she wants to do. I don't need a damned babysitter."

Natalie let out a high-pitched whistle, immediately stopping the verbal battle waging between the two. "Enough already. Mom, what I do is none of your business. If I want to date while I'm here, then I will. I am *not* going back to Steven under any circumstances. Finding him in our bed with another woman sealed the deal for me and there's no going back. Grandma, you need to keep your blood pressure down and stop getting so worked up over things Mom says. You know the two of you can't agree on anything these days."

Both women sheepishly apologized.

"Much better. Mom, why don't you go shopping or something since you obviously plan to stay for a few days, or whatever. I'm going to fix some lunch and then go upstairs to work on some lesson plans I started for the children back home, since I'm not sure when I'm going to teach again for right now. Gram, why don't you go and take a quick nap, and I'll wake you when lunch is ready." Her mother got to her feet, disappearing upstairs without another word. "Come on, Gram, I'll help you into the room down here."

"You're a wonderful woman, Natalie. Have I ever told you that?"

"Thanks, Gram. I love you, and I hope you know I'd never leave you here alone to deal with all of this."

"I know, sweetie, and I love you too. I want you to be happy and find the one man you can love without a second thought."

"I'll find him someday. You just need to stop playing matchmaker."

"No can do, honey. It's in the blood."

"Ah shit!"

* * * *

The next two days with her grandmother and mother at each other's throats at every turn had her on edge. The constant bickering and snapping made her want to pull her hair out by the roots, she hoped the sledding trip with Cade would help smooth those exposed nerves.

Around ten, Cade's truck pulled in the driveway, and her mother cocked an eyebrow when she headed for the door.

"Come on in," she said, pushing open the screen.

He leaned down and brushed her lips with his. The quick inhalation of breath from her mother made her head turn, but the wide-eyed look on her mother's face had her wondering what was going on and why did she look like she'd seen a ghost.

"Mitchell?"

"Uh, no. Mom, this is Cade—"

"Weston," her mother finished for her.

Her mother's face went pasty white, and she sat down in her chair with a thud. "I-I'm sorry. You look exactly like your father, I would assume."

"Mom, do you know Cade's father?"

"You could say so, Natalie. I dated him."

"You what? You dated Cade's father?" she asked, shock reverberating through her. "When?"

"In high-school. I was born and raised here remember? Mitchell, Gerald, and I all went to school together."

Shit! Is Cade's father the 'other man' grandmother mentioned?

The gentleman in Cade wouldn't allow her mother not to at least make his acquaintance. With hat in hand, he stopped next to her chair, holding out his hand. "It's nice to meet you, Mrs. Bennington."

"Yes, you too, young man. I assume your father is well? I haven't seen him in several years."

"He's doin' fine, ma'am."

"Tell him hello for me when you see him again, will you?"

"Of course, ma'am. I'm sure he'll be glad to hear from you."

"Uh, Gram? If you don't need me for a bit, Cade is taking me sledding."

"Very nice," her grandmother replied. "I'm sure you'll have fun sitting between those hard thighs."

Natalie gave up trying to figure out what her grandmother would say next, but the shocked looked on her mother's face was worth any price. "Let me get my coat and we'll go."

"Make sure you put some condoms in your purse, Nat," her grandmother called, and she just shook her head.

"Yes, Grandma."

As Cade followed her down the hall, she could hear her mother asking, "Are those two sleeping together?"

God, Gram, don't...

"Of course, they are, Marie. Good grief; what the hell do you think young people do these days, go out for soda's?"

Ah, hell! "Gram, please!"

"You go on, honey, and have a good time. Don't worry about your mother and me. We'll get pizza for dinner. Cade, you bring her back when you're done."

Heat crawled up her neck, and she turned to find him standing behind her. She couldn't help it. A huge smile spread across her lips, and she buried her face in his shoulder. Her shoulders shook while she tried to calm her laughter. She didn't have to see the look on her mother's face to know her penciled eyebrows were riding her hairline and her lips were pursing in a permanent soured expression.

"It's fine, honey. I love your grandmother. She's a hoot. And I think she's about the funniest person I've been around in a long time."

She raised her head to find his big, baby blues staring right into her eyes. "Good. I love her too. She means the world to me and I can't imagine leaving her."

Did I just say that? I don't want to leave Red Rock?

"I'm glad to hear it. Maybe it means you'll stick around permanently," he replied before kissing her quickly then grabbing her coat to hold it for her.

"I…uh."

"No more talk of staying here, for now. Today, we enjoy the snow and each other. Okay?"

"Sure."

"We'll see you ladies later," he called, ushering her toward the door.

"Wrap that rascal, Cade," her grandmother called, and Natalie about died right there on the spot.

"Got it covered, Mrs. Oliver." His warm chuckled fueled the burn on her cheeks.

"Will you stop, please? You're encouraging her," she whispered out of the side of her mouth. She couldn't stop her own laugh though. "Bye, Gram. Bye, Mom."

"Have a good time, Natalie," her mother replied.

"Oh, and Nat?"

"Yes, Gram."

"The bench seat in his truck might look like fun, but really, a nice soft bed is better. He's a big guy and I'm sure he needs the room."

"Let's go, please. She's killing me here." Natalie giggled. Gasping for breath between laughs, she waved over her shoulder and walked outside.

Snow glistened in the sunlight like diamonds on a blanket of white. She'd almost forgotten how beautiful Montana winters were, but Cade planned to remind her with this sledding trip. They drove to Marshall Hill and found a place to park. Several of the school children apparently skipped school today since the hill seemed crowded.

"Wow. There are lots of people here."

"Not really. This isn't much. You should see it on weekends."

"I can imagine."

Once they stood outside of his truck, he took her gloved hand in his, grabbed the sled from the back, and they started their trek up the hill. It really wasn't a huge rise, but if she remembered correctly, the sledding on it was great—swift and clean. No rocks or trees to worry about and it leveled into an open field.

"Do you want to go down alone?" Cade asked.

"I kind of like grandma's suggestion of being between those hard thighs."

"You sure know how to crank up the heat."

She felt totally wicked. "Heat? You want heat?" Her hand slipped between them and cradled his cock through his jeans. "Oh yeah. Hot and hard."

"You're a wicked woman, Natalie Bennington." He leaned down and nipped at her earlobe. "I want to get you alone so bad, I ache. How about we skip the sleddin' and go back to my apartment?"

Two steps back and she grinned. "Nope. You promised me sledding and sledding is what we're going to do. Saddle up, big boy. Ride 'em hard."

"You're a witch," he growled.

The wicked giggle coming from her lips almost sounded witchy too.

Cade set the sled down and climbed on. "Come on, honey. You wanted between these thighs. You got it."

Her breathing hitched, and her lips dried just thinking of climbing between his legs and wiggling her butt against his cock. The dream from the night before came back in a sharp picture. He was about to slide his hard length into her ass when the phone woke her from it. Now, the images seemed real, causing her nipples to bead into hard nubs.

"You comin'?"

Not yet.

"Mmm. I'd love to."

His eyebrow arched and his lips twitched. One finger crooked in invitation as his smile widened. "Right here, honey."

She crawled onto the sled, slipping between his thighs, wiggling her butt backward until she felt his cock pushing against her ass.

"I want to fuck you there so bad," he growled in her ear. "Tight." He licked her neck. "Hot." Her pussy throbbed as blood rushed in, and she moaned.

"Hey, mister! Move it! Some of the rest of us what to slide down too," a small boy, about ten, yelled, drawing their attention.

"I guess we should get moving, huh?"

"I'm movin' all right," he murmured, grinding his cock against her ass.

"Sledding, Cade, sledding."

"Oh, yeah, right," he replied with a chuckle. He pushed them off the hill, and tucked both booted feet in next to hers. Cold wind rushed passed her exposed ears, stinging her unprotected cheeks. Nothing could compare to the thrill of sliding down the hill at breakneck speed with one of the most gorgeous guys she knew snuggling against her back.

When they reached the bottom, she laughed out loud, jumped to her feet and yelled, "Let's go again!"

The smile on his lips took her breath away when he joined her in laughter. "Okay." He grabbed her hand and they headed back up the hill.

Over an hour later, exhaustion set in. It had been a long time since she'd done this much climbing and walking. "Wow. I'm beat."

"I can imagine. We've been down the hill probably fifty times."

"Not that many," she replied. "Twenty."

"Nope. I'm sure it's at least fifty."

"I need something warm to drink. How about we hit the diner in town and get some coffee."

"Sure. I could use some lunch. I'm gettin' kind of hungry."

"Is it lunch time?" A quick glance at her watch confirmed what she already suspected. "Wow. I didn't realize it was so late. Maybe we should go by the house and check on Gram."

"Why don't you call her? I'm sure everything is fine or your mother would have called you."

"All right. I'll call her while we walk back to the truck."

"Perfect," he replied, tucking her hand in his.

The phone rang in her ear soon after she dialed.

"Hello?"

"Hi, Gram. How are you?"

"I'm fine, honey. How's sledding?"

"It's been great, but now we're heading into town for some coffee and lunch. Can we bring you anything? Are you okay?"

"We're fine. Don't interrupt your fun. Have a good time and don't worry about being home for dinner. I'm sure you'll need some snuggle time to warm up certain parts."

She couldn't help rolling her eyes, and Cade mouthed 'what', but she shook her head in answer.

"I'll be home after while, Gram. Don't kill Mom while I'm out, all right?"

"Of course not, Nat. I only gagged her and tied her up in the basement until you get home."

"You did not!" Her grandmother laughed hysterically. "Please tell me you are kidding, Grandma."

"I'm kidding, Natalie. I've got her tied to the bed in the guest room. Have a good time and I'll see you later." The phone went dead with a click in her ear, and she fought the urge to call back. She stared at the phone for a second, debating.

Cade took the phone from her fingers, stuffing it into her pocket. "She's fine, Nat. Your grandmother is kidding."

"I'm not so sure." She giggled. "My mother is a handful when she wants to be."

"Your grandmother can handle your mother and twenty Marines along with her."

"Very true."

"Let's get lunch and we can swing by the house afterwards," he said, opening the door to the truck.

"All right." Her stomach growled. "I am kind of hungry."

Within minutes, they parked at the diner and took a booth in the back. The waitress came by their table, asking what they wanted to drink.

"Coffee, please," Natalie said, rubbing her cold fingers together.

The woman gave Cade a frown when he took Natalie's hands between his and stroked them over her freezing digits.

"Make it two, Audrey."

"Sure, Cade. I'll be right back."

"Someone you know?" Natalie asked.

"Audrey? Sure. She grew up here too. Why?"

"The dirty look I got."

"What dirty look?"

"When she comes back, you'll see it."

Audrey returned a few minutes later with their coffee and took their order. The anger Natalie saw on the woman's face gave her pause. *Obviously, Audrey has a thing for Cade.*

When she finally walked away, Natalie asked, "Did you ever date her?"

"No."

"Well, she must want you to, by the look in her eyes."

He took a small sip of his coffee and said, "What look?"

"The one that told me she'd meet me in the parking lot on some dark, rainy night to beat the shit out of me, if given the chance."

"You're imaging things, Nat. I have never given her the impression I would be interested in dating her."

"She wants you to though."

Cade grasped her hand in his, squeezing her fingers. "I don't want her. I want you. On the couch, in my bed, in the shower, on the countertop—"

"Enough! You're making me blush."

"I want to make you hot."

"Um, that, too."

"Then I'm doing a good job?"

"An excellent job."

"Will you come back to my place so we can take care of our little heater problem?"

"I can't."

"Can't?"

The tentative shake of her head made him frown.

"Why not?"

"I promised Kale I wouldn't have sex with you again until he's had a chance."

"Chance at what?"

"To woo me, or whatever you want to call it."

"You told me you didn't have sex with him last night."

"I didn't."

"But you had phone sex with me."

"Well, yes, but that's different. It wasn't real sex. I can't have real sex with you again."

"We can have phone sex then?"

She looked at the ceiling and shook her head. "I'll have to clear it with Kale."

"Clear it with Kale? This is ridiculous, Natalie. If we want to have sex, then we should be able to have sex," his voice started to rise, drawing several pairs of eyes to them.

"Please, keep your voice down. I don't really want the whole damned town to know about us."

"They already know about us, Natalie. Watch." He stood and turned toward the crowd. "Folks! Most of you know who I am, but many of you don't know this beautiful lady." His hand swept to her, and she wanted to crawl under the table.

"Cade, please."

"This is Natalie Bennington, and she and I are dating. In fact, we've had sex." Hands clapped and several gentlemen in the place gave him thumbs up.

"Damn it, Cade! I'm walking out of here right now unless you sit back down." She knew her face had to be flaming red, and she wanted to kill him right now.

He slid back into the booth and sipped from his cup.

"How could you do that? You've completely embarrassed me in front of the whole town. I do not believe you!" She made up her mind swiftly, grabbing her purse and sliding out of the booth. "You can eat by yourself, and don't bother to call or come over, because I don't want to see you again."

Tears burned her eyelids, but she didn't care. She had to get out of there and fast.

"Natalie!" he yelled behind her. "Natalie!"

She kept right on moving until she rounded the next corner and saw a cab sitting next to the curb. The door came open with a tug of her hand, and she rattled off her grandmother's address. "Quickly, please."

"Yes, ma'am," the driver responded, flipping the car into drive.

She glanced over her shoulder to see Cade sliding to a stop at the corner then throwing his hands in the air. Tears fell and a sad sob escaped her lips. *I thought he really cared about me, but all he's interested in is showing off in front of everyone. I'll never be able to face anyone in this town again.*

Moments later, her grandmother's house came into view, and the cab pulled to a stop at the curb.

"Five fifty, ma'am."

After paying the driver, she slipped out the door, slamming it behind her. The wetness on her cheeks felt cold, but her heart felt colder. Caring meant getting hurt. How in the hell she came to care about Cade in such a short time, she didn't know, but she didn't like it.

When she walked inside the house, her grandmother asked, "Where's Cade?"

"Still at the diner I would imagine, where I left his happy ass."

"Oops. What did the big jerk do, honey?" Tears started again and she couldn't stop them. "Come here, Nat. Grandma will make it better."

"Where's Mom?"

"Upstairs ruffling through things, just to be annoying."

She slid into her grandmother's embrace and laid her head on her lap as she did when she was a little girl. The scratch of her polyester pants felt rough against her cheek. The gnarled fingers of her favorite person in the world, stroked through her hair, easing the tension and heartache.

"It sucks to love sometimes," her grandmother whispered.

"I don't love him."

"Oh, honey, yes you do, or you wouldn't be so upset right now."

"I can't fall in love with someone inside of a week, Gram. It's not done that way."

"The heart doesn't always follow logic, Natalie."

"But what about Kale?"

"What about him? You don't sound like you care for him the way you care for Cade."

"I feel like I need to give Kale a chance, Gram. I've only been out with him once, and I haven't slept with him."

"Do you want to?"

"I think so." She captured her bottom lip between her teeth, pondering the thought. Did she really want to have sex with Kale? Did she crave his touch as she did Cade's? No, but it felt right to have Kale touch her. "Yes, I'm pretty sure I do. I haven't been with many men in my lifetime, and I sure don't want to settle with one unless I'm positive I don't want anyone else." She pushed herself up and stared into her grandmother's knowing eyes. "What am I thinking, Gram? It's not like Cade has proposed or anything."

"Then have a good time, honey. There's nothing wrong with making sure one or the other of them is the right man for you. Maybe neither is, but you won't know until you give it a chance to develop and bloom." Her grandmother wiped the remaining tears from her cheek.

"You're right. I'm going to ignore Cade for now and focus on Kale."

"What did Cade do to piss you off?"

"He stood in front of everyone at the diner and told them we were dating."

"There's nothin' wrong with that."

"It wouldn't have bothered me at all, but he made sure to mention we had sex too."

"Dumb-ass."

The chuckle spilling from her lips, made her heart feel lighter. "Typical male is more like it. Overbearing, boastful, arrogant—" The jingle of the phone interrupted her words. She grabbed the phone off the end table and handed it to her grandmother. "If it's Cade, I don't want to talk to him."

"You should tell him why you're pissed."

"He knows. Trust me."

Her grandmother answered the phone, winking at her as she said, "Sorry, Cade. Natalie doesn't want to talk to you right now." The nod of her grandmother's head and the smile on her lips, made Natalie giggle. "Sounds like you screwed up royally, boy. You should know better than to get all full of yourself and shoot your mouth off in front of a crowd." She could hear the low murmur of his voice even though she couldn't hear the words. "I don't think you're good enough for her." The tone got louder, and his words more high-pitched. "It doesn't matter what you want, young man. You need to prove to her you're worthy of her love. The stunt you pulled today tells her you aren't. From what she told me, it was immature, cold, and stupid of you. Get used to being alone if you are going to act in such a manner all the time." More loud noises and a few cuss words came through the phone. "Well, she's already called Kale, and he's planning on filling the hole you created. Suck it up, boy, and get a life." Her grandmother didn't wait for him to say another word before hanging up the phone.

"Oh my, Gram! He's going to be so pissed off."

"Who cares? He needs to understand, pulling shit like that is completely unacceptable behavior for a grown man. I can understand a teenage boy doing something so asinine, but he's old enough to know better."

"Very true."

"Stick to your guns, Natalie, and go out with Kale. If nothin' else, it will teach Cade a lesson he won't readily forget. He'll know he can't push you around or act childish in the future."

"I love you, Gram."

"I love you too, girl. I hope you find the happiness you deserve. You know, I would love for you to find a handsome, down home, country boy and settle right here in Red Rock, but I understand you need to do what is best for you."

"I know. I'm not sure one of the men you described exists though."

"Oh, he exists, all right. You just have to find the one right for you. Right now, you have two following you around like puppies on a string. Work it girl, work it!" her grandmother replied, swinging her hips and pumping her fists.

Natalie laughed so hard, her stomach hurt.

"My, my. Aren't we having fun down here," Marie said, coming down the stairs. "What's so funny?"

"Gram was just giving me some man advice."

"Oh?"

"Yeah."

Her mother arched an eyebrow, waiting.

"Don't worry about it, Mom. Cade did something stupid while we were out. Typical man behavior anyway, and I took a cab back here."

"What did he do?"

"Bragged."

"I don't understand," her mother replied, sitting in the recliner across the room.

"It doesn't matter, Mom. He knows he's in deep shit, and Gram gave him a thing or two to think about, so it's over for now." Natalie rose to her feet. "I need to make a phone call, so I'll be in the kitchen."

She dialed Kale's number and waited. Moments later, his gruff voice answered, making her smile. "Hi."

"Hi, Nat. What's up, babe?"

"Not much. I wanted to talk to you for a minute. Are we still on for Saturday?"

"Of course. Why wouldn't we be?"

"I wasn't sure if maybe Cade called you."

"If he did, I didn't get it. I've been in the barn all mornin'. You caught me comin' in for a bite to eat. Was there somethin' specific he might be calling about?"

"Um. No. I told him a little while ago, I didn't want to see him again."

A deep, choking cough sounded on the other end of the line.

"Are you all right, Kale?"

"I'm surprised is all," he squeaked and coughed again. "Man, he must have really screwed up."

"You could say so, yes, but I didn't call to discuss Cade."

"What did you call for then, Natalie?"

"I want to come out to your place tonight, and I want you to make love to me."

Chapter Ten

"Excuse me?" Kale asked, his voice high.

"I want you to make love to me."

"I-uh."

"What's wrong, Kale? Don't you want to?" She hadn't contemplated that he might have changed his mind.

"Well, of course, I do, Natalie, but I thought we agreed to wait until we knew each other better."

"I've decided I know you well enough."

"I don't know what to say."

"Say yes and I'll see you this evening," she said, hoping he wouldn't say no. She needed to do this to make sure her feelings for Cade were real.

"All right. I'll pick you up around six. Work for you?"

"Perfect. See you then." She hung up the phone and turned around to find her mother leaning against the counter. "Hi, Mom." *Shit. How much did she hear?*

"I think we need to talk, Natalie."

"Talk? About what?"

"You dating two men and obviously sleeping with both of them."

"I'm not sleeping with both of them...yet."

"Sit down, honey."

After glancing at the seriousness on her mother's face, she took a seat at the kitchen table. The same table she baked cookies with her grandmother on, did her homework on when her parents were at work, and the same table she had dinner with Kale on.

"Your grandmother informed me she told you about me dating two men in high-school."

"Yes, she did and I don't see a problem with doing that."

"Good. It appears you are taking the same path, to a degree, and a very strange one."

"I don't understand."

"One of the men I dated was Mitchell Weston. The other was your father, Gerald."

"So you chose Daddy over Mr. Weston."

"Not really, no."

"You didn't?"

"I had to marry your father because I was pregnant with you. But I never stopped loving Mitchell." Her mother stood and walked to the window. Natalie wondered what her mother saw—life how it might be if she'd held out for the love she wanted, or maybe the miserable existence she now lived. "I had been dating Mitchell for some time. Your father expressed an interest in me, and Mitchell had become distant. I wanted to make Mitchell jealous and to express his love for me, other than a high school crush."

"So you dated both men."

Her mother nodded and continued, "Your father and I went out several times. Mitchell and I had a huge fight over me seeing your father, but he still refused to tell me he loved me. I felt crushed and alone. Your father comforted me. I liked him, but I wasn't in love with him. We had sex once and you were conceived."

"You had to marry Dad then."

"I guess you could say that yes."

Trepidation rolled down her back as she thought about one possibly sickening thought. "Please, tell me I'm not Cade's sister."

A dry, non-humorous chuckle left her mother's lips. "No, Natalie. You are your father's daughter. Mitchell and I had never made love. I wanted to save myself for our wedding night. The wedding that never came."

Natalie stood, stepped behind her mother, and wrapped her arms around her from behind. "Oh, Mom. I'm so sorry."

"Seeing Cade today brought back all those memories. He looks exactly like his father—the same blue eyes, proud chin, and muscular build." A heavy sigh left her lips. "I found out a piece of information later on that made the whole thing make sense. Mitchell received acceptance to a college out of state. He knew I couldn't go with him, and he didn't want to leave me alone in Red Rock. He thought pushing me away would be the best thing. Mitchell and Gerald were both a year older than me and I still had to finish high school."

"He really did love you."

"Apparently, but by then, I had you and my marriage to your father. I gave my word to love, honor, and cherish until death us do part."

"Is that why you won't leave him, even though he continues cheating on you?"

"Yes. Unless he asks me for a divorce, I'll never leave him."

"Wow."

Her mother turned, and Natalie could see the terrible sadness in her eyes. "I don't want you caught in the same mistakes I made. Make sure you love the one you choose."

"I thought you wanted me with Steven?"

"I didn't realize how miserable you really were with him. When you told me you caught him cheating on you, it was as if my whole life came back to slap me in the face. I couldn't see past my own guilt to realize you needed out. Forgive me?"

"Of course, Mom. I love you."

"I love you, too, Natalie, and I'm sorry I've made such an unhappy family life for you."

"It's fine. I wish we hadn't moved from Red Rock though."

"We had to."

"I know. The plant closed."

"It wasn't only the plant closing. If we had stayed here, I would have thrown everything away to be with Mitchell again." They took their seats at the table, and her mother grasped her hand between hers.

"Seriously?"

"Yes. Right before we left, he and I talked. That's when I found out all the other things, and he admitted he loved me, but he had a wife and children, too, by then. He wouldn't leave them. The vows exchanged with Callindra meant everything to him, and he wouldn't break them."

"Mr. Weston sounds like an honorable man."

The sad smile on her mother's lips, almost made her cry. "You only know the half of it. But I didn't come in here to go into details about my mistakes. You seem to care for Cade."

"I'm not sure, Mom. We're great together, but then he pulled the stupid stunt today. It made me realize I don't really know him at all."

"Mmm," her mother hummed. "I understand you are dating Kale Dunn? I don't believe I know his family."

"Kale and Cade were best friends in school. They remembered me. After Cade rescued me the night I drove in, they've both been paying a lot of attention to me. Things happened between Cade and me the other day, but I haven't had sex with Kale. I plan to rectify the situation this evening."

"Are you sure you really want to?"

"Yes. I may not go through with it, but I need to know. Things started to heat up last night, about the time you called."

"I'm sorry I interrupted you."

"No big deal, Mom. Kale didn't want to take our relationship any further right then, but I was kind of in the middle of teasing him. He's going to pick me up around six. We'll have dinner and go from there. I need to figure out the feelings I have for both of them. I'm attracted to each of them in a different way and it's driving me crazy."

"Follow your heart, Natalie. It won't steer you wrong."

Her mother got up from her seat, kissed her cheek, and walked into the living room, leaving her alone in the kitchen with her thoughts.

* * * *

Six o'clock came and went, no Kale.

What the hell is going on? He's a no show?

No call. No nothing. She tried calling his house, but no answer.

"I don't believe this. I've been stood up."

"You never know. There could be a problem at his place, Nat. Give it some time," her mother replied, absently flipping through television channels.

"Time, my ass! I'm going upstairs to take a bath. He can go to hell," she grumbled and turned toward the stairs.

The doorbell rang and she glanced at the door. *Do I want to answer it knowing it's probably Kale, or do I want to ignore it and climb into a hot bath?*

"Oh hell." The door opened with a tug of her hand on the knob. "What?" she snapped.

No response. There wasn't anyone on the other side of the screen.

Ookay.

She popped the screen door open and stuck her head outside. The screen was pulled from her grasp and a startled shriek slipped from her lips when Cade grabbed her arm, bent at the waist, and hoisting her over his shoulder. She wasn't sure, but she thought she could hear her grandmother's amused cackle coming from inside the house.

"Go get her boys!" Now that was definitely her grandmother.

"Go Kale," Cade yelled, taking off at a dead run toward his truck.

"Put me down, Cade!"

His hand came down hard on her ass cheek. "Hush."

Within moments, he stuffed her inside his truck, climbed in beside her and slammed the door. Kale sat on the other side, sandwiching her between the two of them.

"Move it, Cade, before her mother calls the cops," Kale growled, checking the mirrors.

Cade cranked the engine, shoved the vehicle in drive and squealed the tires as they took off down the street.

"What in the hell do you think you two are doing?" she snapped, while desperately trying to hide the smile on her lips.

"Kidnapping you. What does it look like?" Kale replied.

"You were supposed to pick me up two hours ago."

"I know, babe, but Cade and I came up with this plan instead."

"And what exactly is *this plan* you two concocted, and how does it involve me?"

"We're taking you back to Kale's so we can have a conversation about us."

"Us?" she asked, not sure she wanted to know what they meant by 'us'.

"You, me, and Kale, darlin'."

"After what you pulled earlier, Cade, there is no you and me."

"You're wrong."

"Wrong am I? How do you explain the fact that I called Kale and told him I wanted to come over to his place tonight, and I wanted him to make love to me? Hmm?"

"You didn't fuckin' tell me she said that, Kale," Cade growled, slowing down for a light.

"I figured it all came back to her wanting both of us, Cade."

"Don't talk like I'm not here, damn it!" she yelled. "This is my decision. Not yours."

"Do you want both of us, Natalie?" Kale asked, taking her hand between his.

"I don't know what I want, but you two bullying me into this little rendezvous isn't going to help make up my mind."

The next turn and they were driving down a long, dirt driveway with a large ranch house in the distance. She assumed this was Kale's home.

A large white two story home with a porch wrapping around three sides reflected the florescent light from the barn. Lights burned in the front windows in an inviting gesture to visit. The large structure behind the house looked like the typical Montana barn with huge doors and painted bright red. The pasture to the side of the house held several horses—their gleaming coats a sharp contrast to the white snow beneath their hooves.

"Wow. Nice place."

"Thanks."

She glanced at Cade from of the corner of her eye and asked, "Are you going to let me walk in or are you going to do the caveman thing and drag me by my hair?"

"Don't tempt me," Cade replied, and she stuck her tongue out at him.

Kale opened his door and held out his hand, but she ignored him. He was in as much trouble as Cade for pulling this stunt.

The huge front door mocked her with its inviting oak door when she stepped onto the porch.

"Allow me," Kale said, opening it for her to enter.

"Don't get all gentlemanly on me now, Kale."

"Have a seat, Nat," Cade said with a sweep of his hand.

She took a seat on the couch, and the two of them sat across from her in the matching recliners. Kale's place looked like a typical ranch home. Open living room with leather furniture and wood accented tables gracing the middle, and a huge rock fireplace took up one whole wall. The dining room stood to her left, but remained empty since he lived alone, she assumed. The kitchen looked like something out of a chef show, like Paula Deen or something, with its stainless steel appliances and shiny granite countertops. When she glanced back at her two hosts, her palms started sweating and itching. Having two gorgeous men focus on her might be how wet dreams are made, but she wasn't sure about it right at this moment.

"So what's this all about?" she asked, sliding her palms down her pant legs.

"I told you in the truck…us," Cade replied.

"Care to elaborate on the *us* part?"

"You were furious at me after lunch this afternoon—"

"An understatement, to be sure."

"What I did is inexcusable and I'm sorry. I tried apologizing when I called, but your grandmother chewed my ass."

"I know. I heard."

"Then Kale called me and told me what you said. Well, most of it, anyway."

The scowl he gave Kale, almost made her smile. He obviously didn't like the idea of her sleeping with his friend, no matter what he said before.

"He didn't mention you telling him you wanted him to make love to you."

"What difference does it make?"

"It makes a lot of difference, Nat. I care about you a lot and I'm not sure how I feel about you sleepin' with Kale."

"You told me you didn't care."

"I was wrong. All right? I do care."

"Do we really have to discuss this in front of Kale?"

"Yes. He's part of this. There is a burn between you. It's very apparent to me, but I can't be in a serious relationship with you until you figure out how to extinguish it."

"You're awfully quiet, Kale. What do you think of all this?" she asked, staring into his brown eyes.

"I want you, Natalie. I've never made any excuses or tried to deny it, but if you are serious about Cade, I'll back off."

"What if I said, I want both of you?"

You could hear a pin drop in the eerie stillness settling over the room. The air grew thick with the tension zinging from her to Cade, then from her to Kale. She waited with bated breath for either of them to say something…anything.

"Are you sure?" Cade asked.

"I want to know what it feels like to be loved by both of you at the same time. Then, maybe, I can decide how I want to play this. I know a threesome type relationship can't work, or should I say, won't work in this town. It's too small and with my job as an elementary teacher, it would be impossible. But if you two are willing, just this once, then I'm game."

"I want to be perfectly clear on this, babe. You want Cade and I to both make love to you, at the same time?" Kale stared across the expanse of the living room, a hopeful look on his face. When she glanced at Cade, he wore almost the exact expression, and she almost laughed.

"Yes."

Both of them sprang off the recliners in a matter of seconds and immediately took the seats of either side of her—Cade on her right and Kale on her left sandwiching her between them.

"You'll have to help me out here, guys. I don't have a clue what I'm doing."

"We'll take care of it, darlin'. Don't worry," Cade growled, his voice deep and sexy. His nose nuzzled against her ear and his warm breath sent shivers down her arms. She closed her eyes and parted her lips.

Kale turned toward her so his chest cradled her shoulder and arm. She pulled her hand back, gasping when it brushed his erection.

"All for you, babe." He took her hand, pressing it hard against his long, thick shaft. "God, I want you so bad, I hurt."

"Tell us what you want, Nat," Cade said, one hand cupping her breast as his thumb rasped over her nipple, making it tighten painfully.

She whimpered low in her throat and pushed her breast further into his hand.

"Good?"

"Yes," she breathed.

"Let's get this shirt off," Kale added, starting to unbutton her shirt.

Moments later, both men peeled the silk from her shoulders, leaving her in only her lacy bra.

"Nice," Cade told her. "But it needs to come off too. I want to feel your sexy, pink nipple puckering hard against my tongue."

Kale unsnapped the back of her bra when she leaned forward, and both men pulled a strap off her arms.

"Oh, man," Kale hissed. "I don't think I've ever seen something so perfect." He palmed her left breast, molding it to his touch. "So gorgeous." He pinched her nipple between his thumb and forefinger, and she almost came off the couch as desire zipped from the tip of her breast to her clit. The rough pad of Cade's tongue flicked at her right nipple. The moans spilling from her lips sounded low and coarse. Her head fell back against the couch, and she looked at the two men through her lashes. Cade's light brown hair was such a contrast to Kale's dark locks. Both were amazing, kind, loving, and melt-your-panties sexy. Both had calluses upon calluses on their hands from hard, every day work...honest work, and she'd never felt anything more enticing than two sets of hands on her skin.

Kale brought her face to his and slanted his mouth over hers. His tongue slipped over the seam of her lips, asking permission to invade the dark cavern of her mouth. When she parted her lips for him, he dove inside, sweeping away any and all thought. Every whimper and groan captured in the exchange of tongues.

"Holy hell, that is totally hot watching him kiss you," Cade groaned against her neck.

Hot breath flittered over her cheek as Kale moved toward her ear. Teeth nipped at her earlobe, and she tipped her head to give him better access to the skin of her throat.

Cade's mouth moved to her breast and he sucked the hard tip deep into his mouth. A tortured whimper escaped as he tongued her nipple.

Fingers pulled at the snap near her waist. She didn't know who they belonged to and she didn't care. Cade's mouth disappeared and she bit her lip to keep from calling him back.

The zipper on her jeans came down with a tug, and she heard Cade murmur, "Lift your hips, darlin'."

Cool air hit her skin as her pants and underwear came off her legs. Goose bumps flittered over her flesh, but she wasn't sure if it was from the sharp inhalation of breath from Cade or from the cooler temperatures of the room.

"Open for me, honey. I'm gonna eat you up," Cade said, dropping to his knees between her parted thighs. Two warm hands grasped her hips and tugged her to the edge of the couch cushion. "Oh yeah. Pink, pouty, and perfect."

She couldn't help but laugh at his words.

"What?" he asked, staring up at her. His blue eyes sparkled in the lamplight and a little smile twitched at his lips.

"Nothing."

His face disappeared between her legs, and she groaned when his tongue licked from her slit to the tip of her clit. *Good Lord, I love it when he does that.*

Kale's mouth moved down her chest, capturing the tight nipple in his mouth.

"Ah, God," she moaned and arched her back. With Cade's tongue doing wicked things to her clit and Kale's mouth sucking her nipple it wouldn't take long for her to crawl off the ledge of climax. Her hands balled into fists at her sides as wave after wave of sensations bombarded her body. Need spiked hard and her legs trembled. Whimpers she couldn't hide slipped from her lips.

Cade slipped two fingers knuckle deep into her pussy, and she almost slipped off the couch while she fought the climax hovering just out of reach.

"Easy, babe," Kale whispered. His thumb and forefinger rolled her right nipple while his mouth recaptured her left.

Heat crawled from her toes and burst through her pelvis as she felt everything centering on the mouth sucking her clit and Kale's ministrations on her breasts. Cade's tongue captured the cream sliding from her pussy as he hummed his appreciation against her flesh.

"Oh yeah," Kale groaned while continuing to roll her nipple. "I can't wait to get between those gorgeous thighs."

"I'm thinking you two have too many clothes on," she said, trying to bring her breathing under control.

"Mmm. Me, too," Cade replied. First, his t-shirt hit the floor, then his jeans. Within seconds, he stood in front of her, hard, ready, and oh-so-delicious.

"Your turn," she told Kale. "I wanna see what I've been missing." Kale chuckled and stripped to bare skin, her mouth watering at the sight. "Damn." She scooted closer and wrapped her hand around his girth.

Kale threw his head back and growled low in his throat, with an answering groan coming from Cade.

"Ain't nothin' hotter than watching your woman stroke another guy's cock, but just this once."

"Your woman?" she asked even though she continued to stroke Kale's cock.

"Damn right," Cade demanded. "We'll settle that tomorrow. Tonight is all for you. We are going to make you come so hard, you'll see stars."

Kale removed her hand and took a seat back on the couch. "Now, babe, suck me."

"Demanding. I like it," she chuckled as she grasped him in her hand and scooted closer.

"Wait," Cade said. "On your knees, darlin'. I'm gonna play."

On her hands and knees, with her mouth hovering over Kale's cock, she would be open to Cade's probing fingers. A position she knew she would love.

A cold dollop of lube hit her ass. "Shit! Did you have that stuff in the freezer or what?"

"Sorry, honey. I'll warm it up real fast," Cade replied, sliding a large smear down the crack of her butt and into her tight hole.

"Mmm," she hummed as she took Kale's cock into her mouth and Cade slipped a finger into her ass. Pressure built inside her pussy, making it throb with need.

Cade's tongue danced up her spine as he continued to probe and prepare her for his penetration. Even if she never had a man there, she read enough about it to know there would be some pain, but hopefully some intense pleasure too.

Her head bobbed up and down with each passing stroke over Kale's rock hard erection. His hands fisted in her hair, guiding her to what he liked, teaching her how to please him. Even though they both said this night was for her, she wanted to make sure she pleasured them well, too.

Small kisses and tiny nips accompanied Cade's pass over her back. Shivers raced down her spine with each flick of his tongue and slide of his lips.

Kale's breathing became ragged and sharp. She curled her hand around his balls, stroking and rolling them in her hand, bringing a tortured whimper to his lips. His shaft hardened and pre-cum glistened on the tip when he pulled himself from her mouth. "I wanna come in your hot pussy, babe."

"You ready, darlin'?" Cade asked, turning her around to face him.

She nodded her head once and said, "Tell me what to do."

"Kale, why don't you lay on the floor near the fireplace, and she can straddle you while I slide into her tight ass."

"Sounds like a plan to me," Kale said, moving to the floor and spreading himself out like a sacrificial Thanksgiving dinner. "Ride me, Nat. I want your sweet heat surrounding me."

"Both of you have condoms, right?"

Kale reached into the small drawer of the coffee table and pull out two foil packages. One sailed across the table at Cade, and Kale tore the other open with his teeth.

She trembled in anticipation. Hot, delicious sensations spiraled through her, settling low in her belly.

"Come to me, Natalie," Kale coaxed with a wicked sparkle in his eyes and a come-hither crook of his finger.

Lips parched when her mouth suddenly went dry as she watched Kale, and then Cade, roll the slippery latex over their impressive lengths. Kale's cock was a miniscule bit thicker than Cade's, but Cade's seemed longer, and for a moment, she panicked at the thought of having him inside her ass.

Cade licked her neck and whispered in her ear as if he knew her thoughts and reservations. "It'll fit, darlin'. I won't hurt you. All you have to do is say stop if you don't like it, but I'm thinkin' you're gonna love this."

After a quick, fortifying breath, she scooted across the floor and straddled Kale's hips. He captured the back of her head and pulled her lips to his. The crush of her breasts against his chest did luscious things to her nipples, and she moaned low in her throat. His tongue brushed the seam of her lips, coaxing her mouth to open for him. Tongues danced, entwined and dueled as both speared and retreated. Kale's hand grasped her hips, positioning her exactly where he wanted her. His rock hard erection bumped at the entrance of her pussy and slid in until only the head lay penetrating her folds.

She tore her mouth from his and lifted herself to take him the rest of the way. With a slow, easy slide, the full length of his cock penetrated deep inside her pussy.

"Oh, God," she breathed.

"Ah, hell yeah," he groaned. His legs trembled beneath her and his hands tightened their grip on her hips.

A quick glance at Cade revealed him palming his own cock, a look of pure bliss on his face. Her pussy twitched and pulsed. He obviously enjoyed watching her fuck Kale. "Are you joining us?"

"Right now, darlin'," he replied, moving behind her. "Lean over Kale's chest." Doing as instructed, he opened her ass cheeks, and she could have sworn she heard an almost animalistic growl from his lips. The whole thing made her feel sexy and beautiful. Colder lube landed on her crack, and she sucked in a ragged breath when Cade eased two fingers inside her tight hole. A low hiss escaped her mouth at the penetration and stretching of her ass. "This will help make it easier."

With each movement of his fingers, the vibrations of need spiked higher and higher. Kale rolled his hips, shoving his cock in and out of her pussy in a slow rhythmic motion meant to ease her into Cade's access.

"Oh yeah. Perfect," Cade murmured when she started pushing back against his hand.

"Please."

"Please what, princess?" Kale asked moments before closing his lips over one nipple.

"Cade! Do it, please. I need you."

The head of his cock paused at her entrance and then, slowly eased inside, passing the tight ring of muscles.

"Easy, darlin'."

"Oh, God! It burns."

"I know, honey. It'll pass in a second. I'll go slow."

He continued to push with unhurried firmness, pausing when she hissed at the burn, then moving more and more, until she completely encased him.

"Holy hell," he growled with his lips against her back. "You are so damned tight, honey. I don't know how long I can last."

After a quick kiss to the back of her neck, he must have moved, so he held himself upright because the angle changed and shoved his cock in so far, she could feel the crisp hair at his groin against her butt.

"So full," she sighed.

"You all right, princess?" Kale asked, watching her face for a reaction.

"Perfect, but now you two need to move. I need this. I want it right now."

The tortured sound coming from Cade seemed echoed by Kale as the two of them found a rhythm of movement to bring her to the peak of ecstasy within moments. Heat exploded through her pelvis, making her pussy cream, coating Kale's cock, lubricating his movements. Her pussy quivered and clamped down on the cock riding so deep inside her, she thought for sure he touched her womb.

"Yes, yes, yes," Cade panted behind her with each thrust of his hips. "You are so damned hot and you feel so perfect."

If she thought the first peak of climax blew her mind, the second burst of hot, explosive feelings rupturing inside her, blasted the first climax right out of the water. Stars burst behind her eyelids, and her pussy and ass clamped down on the steely flesh of the two men giving her pleasure. The cry from her mouth didn't sound like any sound she could think of, but she didn't want to think—only feel. They continued riding her hard until first, Kale's groan of completion, and then Cade's echoed in the silence of the living room.

"Are you all right, darlin'?" Cade asked after slowly withdrawing his now semi-erect cock from her ass.

"Mmm. Yeah," she whispered as she lay sprawled across Kale's chest.

"I don't know, Cade. I think that sounded almost like a purr."

"A purr of contentment, I'm thinkin'."

"You think too much, Cade," she grumbled, already half asleep.

"I've got a great idea. Let's all head upstairs to my room, and we can snuggle the rest of the night."

"I don't want to move," she told them.

"I'll carry you," Cade replied, pulling her from Kale's embrace and scooping her up in his arms.

A contented sigh left her mouth and she snuggled to his chest. "Hurry. It's getting chilly now that we aren't creating heat."

"We can always create more," he whispered with a chuckle. He took the steps two at a time even carrying her weight. The muscles of his six-pack abdomen bunched and rolled with each step.

"I don't think so. You two wiped me out," she answered. She nipped at his chest with her teeth and he yelped. "Don't piss me off, mister. I bite." Her laugh turned into a shriek when he dropped her in the middle of the bed.

"Quit hogging the bed, Nat. Move your ass over in the middle." Kale chuckled and whipped the blankets back on the king size bed.

She quickly snuggled into the warm blankets and waited for the two men to get into position. Cade wrapped an arm around her shoulders and pulled her to his side so her head lay on his chest.

"Perfect," he murmured, kissing the top of her head.

Kale's warm body found her back, and he lay one hand across her abdomen, before he placed a kiss her to her shoulder. "Sleep, princess. All will be worked out in the morning."

Her eyes grew heavy with the warm maleness surrounding her, and she drifted off to sleep.

Chapter Eleven

Morning came way too early for Natalie. The warmth at her back and the crisp hair under her cheek told her the experiences of the night before weren't a naughty dream. She really had sex with both Cade and Kale at the same time. The soreness between her legs reminded her of the wild ride they had taken, but she knew it would be a onetime only thing.

"Mornin', darlin'," Cade whispered against her hair.

She tipped her head back and stared into his baby blues. "Morning. I guess it wasn't a dream, huh."

His amused chuckle made her smile. "Nope. Not unless you high jacked me and took me along for the ride." His eyebrows crunched as he frowned. "We need to talk, Nat."

"I know, but can I get some coffee first? I'm not good at negotiations without coffee."

"Negotiations? Is that how you see us? Something we have to work on terms about?"

"Look, Cade," she said, pushing herself into a sitting position. "Up until you kidnapped me from my grandmother's, I didn't want to see you again. Remember? Which, by the way, I will have words with her about, since I know damned well she was involved."

"Keep it down you two. Someone is trying to sleep here."

"To hell with you, Kale Dunn!" she yelled as she scooted off the bed and threw on a t-shirt she found on the floor.

"What did I do?" he grumbled.

"You're guilty too. Both of you. Drag me out here against my will when all I wanted was to figure out whether I really do love you Cade Weston or whether I—"

"Love me?" Cade asked, grabbing her hand and tugging her closer. "You love me, Nat?"

"No, I mean yes, I mean, I don't know, Cade." She inhaled quickly and blew it out in a rush. "I think so. You drive me crazy when we're together, but I can't get you out of my head. I dream about you at night. I want to be near you all the time. I'm jealous when you talk to other women. These are all new things for me. I've never felt like this before and it scares me to death." The soft click of the bathroom door made her realize Kale left. "We shouldn't be discussing this here. This is Kale's home."

Kale poked his head out of the bathroom and said, "No. It's fine. Go right ahead, princess. I know what you and I had wasn't anything compared to what you just described you feel for Cade and I'm thrilled for you two. I hope someday I can find a woman like you who feels those same things for me."

"I do love you, Kale, but only as a friend. Thanks for last night."

"You're welcome, babe. My pleasure. Now get on with it you two. A man needs his privacy." The beaming smile he gave her told her he was completely okay with the way things turned out. Another click and the door closed.

Cade stood and grabbed his jeans from the floor. Kale thoughtfully grabbed all their clothes from the living room while he carried Natalie upstairs the night before. After snapping and zipping himself into his pants, he sat down on the bed and rubbed his palms down his thighs.

"Natalie, darlin'. God, I wish I knew what to say."

Great. I'm in love with a man who doesn't love me. Why am I not surprised things turned out like this. I mean come on! I've been back in Red Rock two weeks, and I'm thinking I love him? This is nuts. She found her clothes and pulled them on with jerking motions. *I need to go home. Back to Oregon. The time spent with him is too much. I can't handle this. I don't want to. I want my simple, nonexistence back where no one pays any attention to me. I have my cat and my lonely life.* A choking sob broke from her lips and a single tear slid down her cheek, but she wiped it away in angry motions.

"It's fine, Cade. I understand. I mean we only got reacquainted a few short weeks ago. I can't possibly think how you would come to care for me in that short amount of time. It's ludicrous."

He grabbed her hand and pulled her down on his lap. "Don't put words in my mouth, honey. I didn't say I didn't care about you. I didn't say I didn't love you, because I do."

"You what?"

"I love you, Natalie Bennington. You've become my whole world and I don't want to return to feeling alone. I made Kale help me kidnap you last night because I couldn't bear the thought of you mad at me. What I said yesterday was completely uncalled for, and I've been kicking my own ass for being so stupid. Your laughter brightens my day. Your smile warms my heart. I want you to stay in Red Rock with me."

"Stay?"

"Yes. Will you marry me, Nat? Marry me and stay with me in my unfinished house up in the middle of nowhere?" The warm chuckle from his lips had her heart singing. "Raise babies with me? And love me until the end of my days?"

She wrapped her arms around his neck and buried her nose against his throat. His unique scent filled her senses and the love she felt for this man, overflowed her heart. "Yes to all those things, Cade. I love you so much. I can't imagine my life without you in it."

The tears returned, but this time they were happy tears. She couldn't believe the man of her dreams had been right here in Red Rock the whole time.

Home. She'd finally come home.

Epilogue

The high-pitched wail of a baby's cry echoed in the clearing, and Cade couldn't help but smile. His first-born. His son.

"Well, Daddy. How does it feel?" Kale asked, pounding him on the back.

"You have no idea."

"I think it's fabulous. My two best friends' have a child together, and I couldn't be happier for you, Cade. When are you two going to have another one so you have a matching set?"

"Ask Nat. I doubt after the fifteen hours of labor she endured, she'll let me near her for a while."

"Yes, well I'm sure, given time, she'll let you back into your bed and not make you sleep on the couch anymore."

"It's about time you figured out how that thing between your legs works, Cade Weston," Mrs. Oliver said from the rocking chair on the porch. "You and Natalie have been married two years now."

He smiled and shook his head before bending down and kissing her on the cheek. "I love you too, Gram."

"God, I hate when you get all mushy on me. I have to keep you in line, you know." Her eyes sparkled as a playful grin spread across her face, and she winked.

The door opened and Marie stepped out carrying a blanket wrapped bundle. "Do you want to see your son now that's he's all cleaned up? The mid-wife is working on Natalie, so it'll be a minute before I suggest you go back in there."

Marie handed him the baby and he pulled back the soft wool from his son's face. "Hey there, little guy? You gave your momma a hell of a night, huh." The baby blinked several times and opened his eyes. "I'm not sure if you're gonna have my blue eyes or your momma's green ones, but your hair is definitely light like hers."

"What did you and Natalie decide to name him, Cade?" Marie asked, taking the seat next to her mother.

"Alan Mitchell Weston."

"It's a beautiful name, and I'm sure your father will be thrilled you've given your son his grandfather's name," Marie said. "I forgot to tell you how sorry I am about your mother's death. I can't imagine the pain your father is going through."

He swallowed hard, fighting the tears of sorrow along with the tears of happiness at the birth of his child. His mother would never get to hold her grandchild in her arms now and it made him very angry. A drunk driver hit her two months ago when she headed home from town. Lucky for her, she died instantly and didn't suffer, but the man who hit her would if Cade had any say in the matter.

"Thank you, Marie. It's been really rough on all of us. I thought for a bit during the whole thing, Natalie might go into labor early, but this little guy..." He kissed the baby's forehead. "Managed to stay put until it was time." The baby started to squirm and screw up his face. "Mmm. I think he needs his mama."

The group chuckled when the baby let out a piercing scream, and Cade hurried into the house to find his wife.

Natalie lay propped up in the bed, dosing quietly when he walked in, but her eyes opened and a beautiful smile graced her face as he approached the bed.

"How are my two favorite men?"

"This favorite man needs a kiss," Cade replied, bending down to brush his lips over hers. The kiss went on for several minutes, and he had to pull himself away to keep from ravishing her right then. "This favorite man needs food I'm thinkin'."

"There you go with your thinking again," she replied with a laugh. "Here. Let me have him. He probably needs to nurse."

Cade's cock twitched in his pants when she dropped the edge of her nightgown and positioned the baby at her breast with a soft 'oh' when he latched on.

"It'll take a bit of getting used to, Natalie, but you'll be a pro in no time," the mid-wife said. "I'll check on you in a day or two. If you have any trouble, call me."

"Thanks, Leslie. You've been a dream."

"You made it easy. Get some rest."

The soft click of the door signaled her departure and he pulled up a chair next to the bed. "How are you feeling, darlin'?"

"Sore and exhausted, but I'm thrilled our baby is healthy."

"Me, too." His fingers danced down her arm and he watched in fascination as the goose bumps rose in their wake. He loved how responsive her body was to his touch.

"What's wrong?" she asked entwining their fingers.

"I'm just sad my mom couldn't be here. I know how much she looked forward to holding her grandchild."

"I'm sorry, Cade, but I'm sure she's watching over us from above and will be at God's elbow looking out for our children while they grow."

He nodded and said, "You know her favorite time of the day always used to be sunrise. She loved to get up bright and early and wait for the sun to creep over the horizon. She used to tell me it made her feel close to God."

"I'm thrilled our son decided to make his entrance into the world as the sun came up over the hills this morning. He's his grandmother's special baby."

"I love you, Natalie Weston."

"I love you too, Cade. May God bless us with many more just like this one," she said, brushing her fingers down the baby's cheek.

"From your mouth to God's ears, my love."

The End

About The Author

Sandy Sullivan is a romance author, who, when not writing, spends her time with her husband Shaun on their farm in middle Tennessee. She loves to ride her horses, play with their dogs and relax on the porch, enjoying the rolling hills of her home south of Nashville. Country music is a passion of hers and she loves to listen to it while she writes, although when she writes sex scenes, it has to be completely quiet.

She is an avid reader of romance novels and enjoys reading Nora Roberts, Jude Deveraux and Susan Wiggs. Finding new authors and delving into something different helps feed the need for literature. A registered nurse by education, she loves to help people and spread the enjoyment of romance to those around her with her novels. She loves cowboys so you'll find many of her novels have sexy men in tight jeans and cowboy boots.

www.romancestorytime.com

Secret Cravings Publishing

www.secretcravingspublishing.com

Made in the USA
Lexington, KY
28 March 2012